Realty Check

Also by Piers Anthony from
PULPLESS.COM, INC.

Volk

Realty Check

by

Piers Anthony

PULPLESS.COM, INC.
775 East Blithedale Ave., Suite 508
Mill Valley, CA 94941, USA.
Voice & Fax: (500) 367-7353
Home Page: http://www.pulpless.com/
Business inquiries to info@pulpless.com
Editorial inquiries & submissions to
editors@pulpless.com

First Pulpless.Com™, Inc. Edition May 1999.
Library of Congress Catalog Card Number: 98-83266
ISBN: 1-58445-000-2

Book and Cover designed by CaliPer, Inc.
Cover Illustration by Billy Tackett, Arcadia Studios
© 1999 by Bill Tackett

Realty Check

Table of Contents

Chapter 1
Chandelle

"Remember, the Realtor warned us the key card can be used only once," Chandelle reminded him. "Don't let that door close before we're inside." They had been married forty years, but she still felt compelled to remind him of details.

"Got it," Penn agreed. The door opened, and they stepped into the house.

It was beautiful. They stood in the living room, gazing at the carpeted floor, the picture window at the side, the couch, chairs, and the large television set. "It's really furnished!" she exclaimed, surprised.

Penn nodded. "The ad did say it was. But I assumed it would be token, or junky. This is all new."

"I hope we can afford it." She paused, then added: "Assuming we want it." But the truth was that she liked it already. It was in the right location and the neighborhood was good. Unless there was something drastically wrong with the house, it would do for their summer.

"The ad said one month's rent free," he reminded her. "If the second month turns out to be exorbitant, we can move out. I wonder why the other prospects turned it down? It couldn't have been the price, if they didn't even know it."

"Even if the price was too high, that free month should have made them stay that long," she agreed.

"And why wouldn't Ms. Dunbar come with us?" he asked rhetorically. "Realtors always show the houses. They want to clinch the sale."

"She said the proprietor left strict orders," Chandelle said. "Prospects have to look at it alone. Maybe the owner doesn't want any sales pressure."

"You know what? We're stalling. We're afraid something's wrong with it, so we're standing here telling each other what we already know, instead of checking out the house."

She nodded. "Yes we are. We had better go ahead and discover the reason this remains open, so at least we'll know."

They moved through the living room to the adjacent small dining room, and the kitchen beyond. Chandelle stood in the center and turned slowly around, while Penn opened the door to the garage and went in. "Hey, there are tools here—and bicycles," he exclaimed. "Mountain bikes. The prior renter didn't clean out all his stuff."

"There was no prior renter, dear," she said, reminding him again. "Nobody wanted to rent."

"Then the owner is storing stuff here," he muttered.

Was he? Chandelle checked under the gleaming kitchen sink. Sure enough, it was equipped with a quality garbage disposal unit. She pulled open a drawer. There was silverware in it, neatly sorted, of good quality. She opened a cupboard. There were assorted canned goods. She went to the freezer. It was well stocked with frozen foods. She recognized the brand names: all top quality, the kind she favored. All unused, with current "sell-by" dates. This could not be an accident. "The rent must be astronomical," she breathed. "If all this is part of the furnishings."

Penn came back into the kitchen, shaking his head. "Those tools have not been used. It's as if the owner set it up to please himself, then changed his mind. And those bikes—brand new, lightweight, in perfect working order. Not cheap equipment. He couldn't have forgotten those."

"The kitchen is completely stocked," she said. "Food included. Even a furnished house does not include that."

"With food?" He opened the refrigerator door. There was a jug of milk, a can of fruit juice, a head of lettuce, packages of cheese, and assorted other items. "We could make sandwiches right here.

This has all the makings I like."

"Yes, there's a loaf of bread in the breadbox," she agreed. "Fresh today, and the kind we prefer. So we know it isn't accidental. The owner must really want to rent this house."

"Maybe when the others turned it down, he decided to make it more appealing. But it's a nice enough house regardless. Why would anybody turn it down, without even taking the free month?"

They kept coming back to that. She was as mystified as he. She went to the stairway to check the bedrooms, while he went out the back door.

She paused at the base of the stairway. There was a small picture, or plaque, on the wall there. On it was inscribed a simple circle. Did it have a purpose? She would have to call it to Penn's attention. She went on up the stairs.

She was hardly surprised to find the master bedroom set up, its bed neatly made, the top sheet turned in the manner of a hotel room setup. She checked the closets: sure enough, there were suits in one, dresses in the other. There was linen in the linen closet, and socks and underwear in drawers.

On an idle fancy, she took down a hanging dress and tried it on over her own. It fit her almost perfectly. She tied the sash and buttoned the blouse, then tugged the hem straight. She walked to the master bathroom and looked in its wall-sized mirror. Yes, were it not for the slight lumpiness occasioned by the clothing beneath, this would be a perfectly useful and attractive dress. Certainly as good as the rack items she normally bought.

She returned to the closet and looked below. There were shoes: men's under the suits, ladies' under the dresses. Could they possibly fit? They looked as if they might. Yet shoe sizing was a personal thing; every foot was different. A perfect fit was unlikely to be by chance.

This was getting scary. Coincidence could hardly account for it. Someone wanted the two of them here. She was beginning to appreciate why the other prospects had been scared away. This was too much like the spider inviting the fly into its parlor.

Then she became aware of a noise. It was a measured beating or pounding, as in someone banging against a wall.

Suddenly she was frightened. Penn! Where was he?

She ran down the stairs to the kitchen. The sound was coming from the back door. She hurried to open it.

There stood Penn, looking abashed. "Honey, come out here a moment," he said. "But prop open that door."

"Whatever for? We don't want to let the bugs in. And why didn't you just come back in yourself? Did the door lock?"

"Not exactly. Just come out."

She hauled a kitchen chair across and propped the door open. Then she stepped outside. And stood amazed.

She faced what looked like an endless forest. Large old trees were everywhere, extending as far as she could see. "But this is in the middle of the city," she protested somewhat inanely. "The back yard *can't* be this big!"

"Now turn around," he said tightly.

Obediently, she turned. And gasped. The house was gone. There was only a boulder there—with the propped-open door in it. Beyond it she could see the forest, extending endlessly, in all directions.

"I walked all the way around that rock," Penn said. "There's nothing but forest here."

"But—but it's a two story house. It can't possibly fit inside that stone. And the city—where's the city?"

"Now we know why the other prospects turned it down," he said. "I'm just glad I had the wit to pound on that rock."

"I'm glad too," she said weakly. "Penn, there is something very strange here."

He made a droll face. "You're telling me?"

"Upstairs, the bed's made. There is linen, and clothing. In fact—" She paused, realizing that she was still wearing the dress she had been trying on. “There is clothing. I tried on a dress.”

“And it fits,” he said, recognizing the unfamiliarity of the outfit.

“Maybe we should go in and try on the shoes,” she said.

“Maybe we should.” For he knew as well as she did that shoes were highly individual.

They entered the boulder, which was the house, inside. Penn paused to poke his head back out, while holding one hand up inside, verifying that the house was larger inside than out. “I can see out,” he reported, “but not in. There’s no window on the outside.” He wiggled his fingers inside. Then he reversed, looking out the door window while wiggling his fingers outside. They showed clearly. He shook his head, bemused.

Chandelle knew Penn would never rest until he fathomed that mystery, as well as that of the forest itself. But right now he was working on her mystery, and in a moment he moved clear, removed the chair, and carefully closed the door.

They went upstairs to the bedroom. Then she took a pair of lady shoes, and he took a pair of man shoes, and they sat beside each other on the bed and tried them on.

They fit. Chandelle didn’t know whether to feel satisfied or alarmed. “How can this be?”

“It is possible,” Penn said. “Maybe we were targeted. Maybe they wanted healthy uncommitted retirees in their sixties. We made an appointment to come today. These days nothing is truly private. They could have known our sizes. Is that alarming?”

“Is it?” She wanted the reassurance of his logic.

He nodded. “Yes, I think it is. I would rather be anonymous, until I know what’s going on. It is evident that I’m not. Have we plumbed the depth of the strangeness of this site, or is there more we need to know?”

“If it’s a spider luring a fly, would it show the fly the strangeness?”

Penn put the shoes carefully back in their places. "This seems entirely too elaborate for anything inimical. Why didn't the spider simply grab the other prospects before they could leave?"

"Because the Realtor would know, and stop showing the house." Still, she was allowing herself to be reassured.

"I think it's selective, but not inimical," he said. "The proprietor is looking for folk who find a house like this appealing." He glanced at her. "Do we find it appealing?"

She considered. "The layout is nice. The facilities are nice. The location is ideal. Yes, it is appealing. But it scares me."

"Maybe it's supposed to."

"*Supposed* to?"

Penn spread his hands in the way he had, to indicate the shaping of a concept. "Suppose, for the sake of argument, that the proprietor wants a certain type of occupant. One canny enough to recognize the oddity of the site, and nervy enough to use it. So stupid or timid applicants need not apply."

"Then he wants you and not me," Chandelle said with a forced shudder.

"I don't think so. There's the house *and* the yard. That forest scares me, because I know it's impossible, but fascinates me for the same reason. Just as you caught on to the targeting of the food and clothing, which frighten yet intrigue you. He wants you too."

"But the house is ordinary. Scary only because of all the things it provides that Scrooge never offers. It's that forest that's impossible."

Penn reconsidered. "Well, maybe it wants folk who feel challenged by the impossible. But I won't stay without you. So the house has to make things nice for you, too."

Now Chandelle reconsidered. "Suppose the house is just as strange as the yard? Only we haven't seen the impossible aspect yet?"

"Then we'd better find out. We don't want to make a mistake

either way."

They went downstairs and poked around more thoroughly. There was a den with a computer, so Penn turned it on. Chandelle watched over his shoulder. She had never quite gotten the hang of computers. In a moment the screen lighted, with a printed message. PLEASE SELECT DESIRED OPTION. Below was a list of programs, some of which she recognized. "This is pretty fancy," Penn said. "It seems to have a choice of about six operating systems, and it's very fast." He chose one, and it took over the screen.

She didn't inquire how he knew its speed. "Can it do letters?"

"Oh, yes. And it can surf the Internet. And more. This is too big for us; we need a teenager."

"Well, we will have one to entertain. Would this hold Llynn?" For Llynn was their elder granddaughter. They had come to this city in order to be near enough to take her off her family's hands for a while, because she was a handful at fifteen.

"It might, for a while. But I think she's more of a video freak."

"Next stop," she said, smiling. He shut down the computer. They went to the living room, where she turned on the TV set. It came on to a local station. She found the remote control and flicked through the channels. They were endless, and all were quite clear. This must be on a superior cable or satellite service. Some were even foreign language. "Couch potatoes and wild teens will love this," she said, turning it off.

Now she noticed that there were book shelves lining the walls. She went to look at the books, and saw that a number of her favorite titles were there. She saw a sound system, with a small library of compact disc albums. Some of her favorite music was there. There were pictures around the room. All of them appealed to her taste. "This proprietor is good," she murmured. "He has done his homework." But this, too, sent a quiet chill through her. Why should anyone study them so carefully, and offer such a phenomenal house, free?

Penn examined the window. It showed a scene of a weird alien landscape. "This is odd," he murmured.

As if they hadn't encountered oddity enough already! She joined him. "It must be a painting behind glass. A true window would look out on the dull wall of the adjacent building. And no window on Earth would look out on a scene like that."

"But this one does. Try moving back and forth, and you'll see the perspective shift."

"They have three dimensional pictures now, holographs, that show perspective."

"I don't think this is a holograph." He went and rummaged in the garage. He returned in a moment with a long flashlight. He shone it through the window. The light passed through the glass and splashed across the sill, touching the dark earth beyond. A spaghetti shaped plant turned several strands to catch the light better.

"Point made," she said. "That thing is alive and aware."

"And it doesn't grow on this world, I think."

She felt a chill. "I agree. I think the window is sealed because the air out there isn't breathable. Not by us."

"Not by us," he agreed. "It must be a special animation, but a sophisticated one." He gazed at it a moment more, then glanced down. "What's this?" He indicated a panel beside the window.

"Air conditioning control?" But it didn't look like it. It had numbers 1 through 0, and a bar. A tiny screen showed the number 14.

He touched the key labeled #1. Nothing happened. Then he touched the ACTIVATE bar below. The number changed to 1. The window scene changed. Now it was a dark sky filled with stars. In the foreground was a great moon. It wasn't Earth's moon.

They stood and gazed out, awed by the depth and power of the scene. "I don't recognize those constellations," Penn said.

"That moon is moving against the stellar background," Chandelle pointed out. "This is either a remarkable animation, or another actual scene."

"Maybe it's more cable TV. But then, how to explain that plant we just saw react?"

"Try another setting."

He touched #2, and the bar. A seascape appeared, with the waves surging across the rocks in the foreground. One large wave came, and its spume spattered against the window and slid down.

"This is something I shall want to explore farther," Penn said. He touched #1 and #4, and the bar, returning the scene to the original setting.

"Should we try the other panels?" she asked.

"Other panels?"

"The one beside the back door. And the front door."

"I hadn't noticed." He walked to the back, and she followed. There was the panel she had seen. It was set at #6.

Penn touched #7 and the bar. The forest changed. It had been large oak trees; now it was large pines.

"I've just got to check that," he said.

"I will guard the door. Don't go out of sight."

He opened the door and stepped out. She watched him go to the nearest pine tree. He reached out and touched it. But she already knew it was real, for the faint pleasant scent of pine sap and rotting needles wafted in. This was the confirmation that the scene really had changed. It wasn't just an illusion.

She saw Penn try to rip off a piece of bark, but it resisted his effort. So he bent to pick up some fallen needles, and came up with nothing. Why was that? He found a low twig and tried to pull some live needles from it, but couldn't. He turned and walked back to the house, a thoughtful expression on his face.

"I can't budge anything," he said as he entered. "I can see it, feel it, smell it, but not affect it. I almost thought that pine bough was swaying slightly in the wind, but I couldn't move it at all. Not half an iota."

"I saw. It's as if you aren't really there."

He laughed. "It's there, for sure! But I'm not. I'm a ghost." He turned to the panel, and moved it to #8.

This time the forest seemed to be formed of giant ferns, each the size of a tree. He shook his head and touched #9. The landscape became barren rock, with an ugly mountain in the background. #10 brought a scene that looked like molten lava.

"Turn it back!" Chandelle said, alarmed.

He hastily touched #4 and hit the bar. That was a modern city scene.

"You got the wrong number," Chandelle said nervously. But now she wasn't quite sure which was the right one.

He tried #5. That was an ugly plain of brush and tree stumps. He touched #6, and the oak trees returned.

They stared at each other. "This is really strange," Penn said.

Chandelle didn't care to advertise how foolishly alarmed she had been when they almost lost the original setting. "We had better try the front door knob," she said tightly.

He tilted his head. "Are you sure you're up to it, dear?"

"I don't dare avoid it. If the front changes too—" She shook her head, not finishing. This nice house had become frighteningly complicated.

They went to the front. That number was #73. Penn reached slowly for the panel, visibly set himself, and reset it to #74. They peered out the pane.

The city had changed. It remained a metropolis, but the street and buildings across it were different.

"More?" Penn asked.

"Turn it back."

He touched #73, and the familiar street returned. He withdrew from the panel as if it had become hot. They retreated to the living room couch and sat down. Penn put his arm around her back, and Chandelle put her head into his shoulder and cried. It was her way of handling extraordinary tension.

After a bit she disengaged. She had recovered some of her equilibrium. She dug into her purse for a hanky and patted her face. "What do you think it is?"

"Something well beyond anything we know." He looked shaken. "So maybe those are all images outside, with enough play to really seem real. But I don't think so. I think they're real. Which means this house is something really special. Whoever built it has technology we've never seen."

"But why?" she asked plaintively. "Why do all this, and just set it out for rent?"

"I'd sure like to know. Oh, would I like to know!"

She nerved herself, and spoke. "There's only one way to find out."

He nodded. "Rent it."

"Do you want to?"

"Honey, I don't want to upset you—"

"You want to rent it. Because we had a deal: one month in the city, with its culture, the way I like it, and then a month in the wilderness, roughing it, the way you've always dreamed. That's all available right here, depending on the door we use. And we have undertaken to take Llynn off her family's hands for a while. I think this house will interest her, and that's two thirds of the battle. Maybe she'll forget to be so wild."

"Yes. I have the feeling that everything we have known in life so far pales into insignificance beside this. We are being offered a chance to explore—to investigate, perhaps, the universe." He looked at her, the doubt manifest. "But do you really want to?"

She took a deep breath. "Definitely. Remember, my name means 'Candle.' It is better to light it, than to curse the darkness."

He kissed her. "I can't say you won't regret this."

"I know. But I'm curious too. And the first month's rate is right." She got up and walked to the phone. As she brought the receiver to her ear, she heard the beeping of automatic dialing. A programmed phone?

"Dunbar Reality, Karen speaking." It was their Realtor.

"Chandelle Green here. We're at the house. We want to rent."

"Excellent. I was afraid you wouldn't. But do you mind telling me—"

Chandelle avoided that by interrupting her. "This house has everything! The owner forgot to remove—"

"No. It is stocked for your convenience. Everything there is for you to use. Come to the office and we'll give you the permanent key."

"Thank you," Chandelle said faintly. "We'll be right there." She hung up the phone. "It's done. We just have to pick up the regular key. And we can use everything."

"I wonder what we're in for?" Penn asked rhetorically.

"What, indeed!" Her heart was beating rapidly.

Chapter 2
Penn

Penn felt a private thrill of excitement and anxiety as they used one of their two permanent key cards. They had made their commitment, for one month, but had they done the right thing? This house was the strangest he had encountered, and he had been around the world during his days of active military service. It looked so ordinary on the outside, but it was an alien structure. That picture, that forest—what else was there to discover?

Tonight would be their first here. He wasn't sure he would sleep well, and worried about Chandelle. But they had to do it. They had to establish their temporary residence here, braving the unknown for the sake of the challenge it offered.

"You go on in," he told her as the door opened. "I'll take the car around to the garage, and you can buzz me in."

She nodded, her lips tight. "Don't be long, dear."

"No dallying on the way," he agreed, forcing a smile. He did not want her alone in that house any more than she wanted to be alone in it. Not yet.

He walked back to the car, got in, and started it. The seat belt alarm sounded. That was an indication of his nervousness, because he always buckled up before inserting the key. This time he had forgotten. He fastened it, then drove down and around into the short driveway leading to the garage door.

As he approached, the garage door rolled up. Chandelle had wasted no time; he had expected a wait of a few seconds while she made her way through the house and into the garage.

He pulled in and parked as the overhead door rolled down behind. He got out, and saw Chandelle at the inner door. "Oh, you're already in," she said.

Penn paused. "You didn't let me in?"

"No, I just got here. How did you open the door?"

"I didn't. It rolled up as I came near. And down behind me."

"Your key!" she exclaimed. "It sensed it, and it's automatic."

"That must be it," he agreed, relieved.

He unloaded the car while she got busy in the kitchen. They didn't have a lot; they had learned to make do on the move. With this house as well stocked as it was, they would need even less.

That reminded him of that aspect. Why should the proprietor be so eager to have them stay that he not only provided a month's free rent, but also food, clothing, and equipment? Was there some phenomenal liability lurking?

He carried a bag up the half stairs. He noticed a little plaque on the wall where they merged with the flight upstairs. It was simply a vertical line, or the number 1. To indicate that this was the first floor? In a two story house, with basement and no attic? It hardly seemed necessary.

He thought about going outside again, to explore one of the back yard scenes, and decided against it. They had had enough mystery for one day.

Soon enough they had dinner in the dinette alcove. Chandelle had done a good job, as usual. Rich black bean soup with rice and salad. And a small glass of wine. That was another signal of her nervousness. They were light drinkers, but it did tend to steady her nerves.

He raised his glass. "To a great experience," he said.

She matched him. "To an enjoyable summer."

After dinner he set things up the way they liked them, with their popular magazines to read while they watched *TV: New Scientist* for him, *Reader's Digest* for her. She took care of the dishes quickly, using the state of the art kitchen equipment, and joined him in the living room. Soon they were watching a good movie, not deep but funny, exactly what they needed to relax. This resembled pay-per-view, with no commercials, but they seemed to have it prepaid.

They retired to the bedroom after ten. This, too, was a signal: Penn had been an early bird all his life, so naturally he had married a night owl. Normally he was asleep hours before Chandelle retired, and was up hours before her. They had worked it out over the years and were comfortable. For one thing, it gave them time alone, and that was important in a long term marriage. It also extended their hours of alertness. A burglar who wanted to break in unheard and unseen would have to do it in the wee hours only. But he suspected that no burglar could get into this house. Like a well trained police dog, the house surely had its deadly aspect. And that was most likely what concerned Chandelle. So she did not want to be alone, here, yet. When that phase passed, in a few days, they would be truly settled in.

He read his material, and she read hers, and soon he slept. He woke briefly in the night, needing to use the bathroom, and Chandelle's light was out, so he knew she had managed to sleep too. They had become accustomed to sleeping in new places, because of the military habit of moving personnel frequently; it was just this house that was odd. But he liked it, and had the gut feeling that its oddity represented much less of a threat than a challenge.

He woke at six, as usual, and got up and washed and dressed in the near darkness, letting Chandelle sleep. Normally he took an early morning jog for aerobic exercise, and worked out a bit with hand weights, keeping himself in shape. But he did not feel easy about leaving the house by either door, until his wife was up and about. So he went downstairs, jogged in place, and used the weights. He also brought out his compound bow and stretched the string several times. Later in the day he would set up his target in back; it would be a novel setting, that primeval forest.

He fixed his own breakfast, took his vitamins, and tuned in *Morning Edition* on his portable radio. All he was missing was the morning newspaper.

Or was he? He got up and went to the front door. There on the front step were two different newspapers. He fetched them in. Sure enough: one was the kind he liked, with sports and national and international news, while the other was the kind Chandelle liked, with local features and advice columnists and crossword puzzles. She would be pleased.

In an hour she came down to join him. "I got to sleep too early," she muttered, and put on her coffee.

"I thought I'd jog outside, but—"

"Not yet," she said quickly. "Let's get Llynn first."

So there would be one more person in the house. That way Chandelle could go out shopping, and he could go out jogging, and someone would still be minding the shop. It was a sensible precaution, in a new neighborhood.

In due course Chandelle phoned the Wiley residence: their married daughter. "We can pick up Llynn in an hour," she said into the phone. There was a pause. "Yes, but I think she will like this house we're renting."

"We'll tell her she can go home tomorrow, if she doesn't like it today," Penn said.

"Yes, it's a very nice house," Chandelle said into the phone. "I do believe Llynn will want to stay." There was another pause. "An hour, then. We'll see you. Bye." She hung up.

Penn smiled. "I notice you didn't give much detail on the house."

"Who would believe it?" But it was more than that, and they both knew it.

They went to the garage, got in the car, and started the motor. Sure enough, the door rolled up on its own. Chandelle was at the wheel; she nodded, and backed carefully out. The door rolled down after them. "It is a very obliging house," she remarked. "But I think it will be the back yard that Llynn first notices."

"I think so," he agreed. "I'll offer to take her on a hike."

"And she will expect to be bored out of her gourd."

They chuckled and lapsed into silence. This was one time the old fogies expected to have the last laugh.

Llynn was standing out front with her bags as they pulled up. She was a rather pretty young woman of fifteen, with glossy black hair that reached almost to her waist and a slender but filling figure. She wore a light blouse that was somewhat too tight, and a dark skirt that was somewhat too short.

"She's growing up," Penn remarked.

"That's the problem," Chandelle reminded him.

They stopped at the curb, and Penn got out to help the girl with her baggage.

"I can handle it myself, Grandpa," Llynn said, opening the trunk and dumping her bags in. Then she got into the back seat.

"We should check with your parents," Chandelle said.

"They know where I'm going," the girl retorted. "And I won't be there long."

Chandelle started the car without replying. She was leaving the dialogue up to Penn, preferring to be officially uninvolved. She knew what was coming.

"This sounds a bit like hostility," Penn said, glancing back as they moved into the flow of traffic.

Llynn turned an exaggerated wide-eyed stare of mock innocence on him. "What, hostility, Grandpa? Whatever gave you that idea?"

He smiled, facing forward again so that they were not looking at each other. "Oh, it was just a silly guess."

"Just because I'm wearing lipstick and dating the leader of the band, my folks want to pack me off to Siberia. Why should I be hostile?"

"And how old is this band leader?"

"Twenty five," she said grudgingly. "But it doesn't matter. He's a great guy."

"Surely so," Penn said. "Old enough to know the definition of statutory rape."

"You folk don't have any idea about anything!" Her vehemence suggested that the term had scored. "Well, I made a deal with Mom: I stay one week with you, then I'm home again. I don't have to pretend I like it."

"I'll make you another deal," Penn said evenly. "You stay one night with us, with an open mind, and if you don't like it, you can go home this time tomorrow."

"Mom wouldn't let me."

"She will if *her* mom tells her."

There was a pause. Llynn was evidently waiting for Chandelle to object, but she didn't. "Where's the catch?"

"No catch. We just think you'll like it with us."

The girl sighed. "Grandpa, it's not you. You and Grandma are okay. It's that I don't like being manipulated. I've got my own life to live."

"We understand that. We think we can show you a better life. We want you to recognize that, so that there's no quarrel between us."

"In one day?"

"In one hour. Deal?"

"Deal."

They drove on in silence. Penn glanced at Chandelle without turning his head. There was a trace of a smile on her face. She knew, as he did, that Llynn had always been an adventurous girl, really a tomboy, until the past year. If that backyard forest didn't inspire her, nothing would. Llynn was smart, and liked to unravel mysteries. She was about to discover a big one.

They arrived at the house, and approached the garage. It let them in. "Chandelle will show you your room," Penn said. "Then come out back for your hour with me."

"The hour that will show me a better life," Llynn said. She was trying to be sarcastic, but her curiosity was getting to her. She knew he didn't bluff, but she evidently couldn't figure out what he might have in the back yard.

Penn stood gazing out the window section of the back door while woman and girl went upstairs. Then Llynn returned. She had not changed her clothing. "I'm from Missouri," she said. "Show me."

He glanced back, and saw Chandelle coming down the stairs. He caught her eye, and she nodded. She would be alert for their re-entry. That meant he could close the door.

Without a word, he opened the door and ushered Llynn out. She went before she looked. He followed, and closed the door behind them.

She paused, staring ahead at the massive trees, and the forest extending to the horizon. "I thought this was in the city."

"It was."

She turned to face him—and her eyes widened. "Where's the house?"

He gestured at the boulder that was where the house should have been.

"I have to admit this is some trick, Grandpa! It's screened out?" She stepped close to the boulder, tapping the rock. "Feels real."

"Let's walk around it," he suggested.

"You can't walk around a screen. I mean, if you do, the illusion vanishes."

"I agree." He set out walking around it.

She ran to catch up. "This forest—it's everywhere! In front, too."

"So it seems."

"And the boulder—there's no screen." She found a place and scrambled up the side, heedless of her flaring skirt. She went to the top. "It's real!"

"It's real," he agreed.

She turned around, scanning the forest. "No city at all."

"No city," he agreed.

She jumped down the far side. He walked on around to rejoin her. They completed the circuit.

"A three-dee video projection," she said. "But I sure can't figure where the house went."

"Maybe the trees are just an image," he suggested.

"I wonder." She dodged to the side and ran out to the nearest tree. She touched it. She walked around it. Then she went to another. "Something funny about these trees."

"Yes. I was unable to break off even the smallest twig."

She located a tree with low branches. But the lowest was still just out of reach. "Boost me up, Grandpa. I want to get a taller view."

"In that skirt?"

She paused. It was clear that she would have to hike her skirt up over her hips to climb the tree, and that he would have to put a hand on her bottom to boost her up to the first branch. "Maybe I better change."

Penn shrugged. He had made his point.

"Wait here, Grandpa!" She dashed toward the boulder. Then she stopped, "Oops."

"Just go where we were, and knock," he called.

She did so. In a moment the door opened out, resembling a section of stone. She ran in, and it swung closed.

Then in a moment it opened again. Chandelle's head came out. "Good thing you didn't boost her," she called.

"It would have been fun."

She stuck her tongue out at him, then retreated.

In another minute the door opened once more, and Llynn charged out. Now she was in blue jeans and a long-sleeved plaid shirt, and her hair was bound back into a long pony tail. She had done a lot in a hurry.

She ran back to join him. "Now," she said, flushed with excitement.

She lifted her right foot, and he linked his hands to make a stirrup for it. She stepped up, and he lifted her foot to waist height as she grabbed onto the trunk of the tree. Then she dug her feet into the trunk, and he set both hands on her bottom and pushed her up another eighteen inches so that she could reach the branch and get a good hold. He waited below as she scrambled to get her feet up on it and work her way to the upper side. He was ready to catch her if she fell, just as he had been when she was six. But she remained athletic, and soon straddled the branch.

She peered down at him. "Aren't you sorry you made me change?"

"I'm your grandfather, you impertinent vamp!"

"You're sorry," she said.

Indeed, it would have been a sight, and a feel, in the skirt. But old men weren't supposed to notice such things. Especially not in connection with their own grandchildren. "Just watch your handholds."

"Got it." She proceeded to climb on up, from branch to branch, as the limbs were closer together there. Soon she was scarily high. She was still a tomboy, now that she was dressed for it.

When she got so high that he couldn't see her because of the intervening branches, he began to be uncomfortable. How could he know where to catch her, if she fell? And from that height, *could* he catch her? She was no giant, but she weighed perhaps 110 pounds, and that was more than he could handle if it came at him with any force. Yet he would have to try.

But she wouldn't fall unless a branch snapped unexpectedly, and these branches would not give way at all. So she was probably safe.

Then she was coming down. He heard her before he saw her. When she was about twenty feet from the ground, she stood on a branch and spread her hands as if about to do a swan dive. "Catch me, Grandpa!"

"Don't jump, you idiot!" he cried.

She laughed as she resumed her descent. "Gotcha that time, didn't I."

She had, indeed.

She reached the lowest branch, then swung below it, hung by her hands, and waited for him to clasp her legs and ease her to the ground. He had to slide her down across his body, face to face, and her shirt tore out before her feet were all the way down. He averted his face before her descending bra collided with it.

She laughed as she put herself back together. She knew she had been naughty. “It’s payback, Grandpa.”

“Payback?”

“For winning the bet.”

“Bet?”

“I’m not going home tomorrow.”

Oh. “Then you can help us figure it all out. There’s a lot more to that house than this.”

“I’m game. Tell me about it.”

“This isn’t the only setting.”

“Setting?”

“There’s a panel by the door. It changes scenes.”

“And this is just one scene? This I must see.”

They returned to the boulder. The door opened. “I saw you two roughhousing out there,” Chandelle said with mock disapproval.

“Oh, not to worry. Grandpa didn’t fondle me much.”

Penn ignored that. “This is the panel. Try punching numbers.”

She looked, and saw the #6 on the panel. She touched 5. The ugly plain with tree stumps appeared.

“They cut it all down!” she cried, horrified. “That beautiful forest!”

Penn hadn’t thought of that. #5 was the future of #6? “Could be.”

She touched 4. The modern city scene appeared. “That’s not here! Not Philadelphia! I would recognize the horizon.”

“So it’s not just countryside,” he agreed. He had not recognized the city either. “And it doesn’t align with the front door.”

“I guess not,” she agreed, not understanding his import.

She touched 3. A futuristic city appeared, with buildings formed into graceful escarpments, and suspended walkways between them.

"This is time travel!" she exclaimed. She was one quick study, once a subject had her full attention. She touched 2.

This was a scene of desolate destruction. Only the ruins of buildings showed, and nothing lived. "After World War three." She touched 1.

Now there was an alien village there, with contours that made no sense for human habitation. "And after we obliterate ourselves, the aliens move in and start anew," she concluded. She glanced at Penn. "And the higher numbers go into the distant past?"

"Yes. Back to the original lava flows."

"Wow!" She touched 6, restoring the oak forest. "There's more? I mean, elsewhere in the house?"

"Yes."

She walked to the next room and picked up the phone. She dialed a number. "Mom? Pack the rest of my things. I'm going to be here forever." There was a pause. "No, it's no joke. This house—" She glanced at Penn, who shook his head. "Is fascinating, with a really nice yard. I'll pick my stuff up tomorrow." She hung up, surely leaving her mother amazed.

"It seems best not to advertise what we have here," Penn said, a bit lamely. "Until we understand it better."

"Got it. Let's go out and explore that forest. I want to know how far it goes."

"There are mountain bicycles in the garage. We could loop around several miles before dark."

"Great! Only keep Grandma inside to open the door."

He nodded. "That's one reason we wanted you. To have a party of two to explore, without leaving the house empty."

"Got it. Let's go."

That quickly, it was decided. They got the bicycles, loaded

knapsacks with spot supplies, and headed out. "Be home before dark, you kids!" Chandelle warned them.

"Yes, ma!" Llynn replied.

"Yes, ma," Penn echoed. They laughed, sharing the generational joke. It was good to have rapport, rather than opposition. Llynn had been set for hostility, but the house and its settings had demolished that.

They rode along a contour, generally west. When they lost sight of the house, they paused, and Penn brought out some bright elastic tape and put a band around a tree. They intended to follow the sun, but to provide a return trail too, so as to be very certain not to get lost. They did not want to get caught out here at night.

They continued, banding trees spaced so that the last band was always in sight from the current one. That meant that from any given tree, they should be able to see the bands both forward and back. They would verify that on the return trip.

The bikes were good. They had the wide tires that handled sand and turf, and the level handlebars that facilitated power without forcing an unrealistic hunch. With fifteen speed settings, they had no trouble finding what was comfortable.

"You know, this is fun," Llynn said as they paused for another banding.

"Exploring the unknown?"

"That, too. I mean, just being out here with you, Grandpa, doing something. The way we used to, when I was a kid. I thought it'd be dull as dishwater, but it's not."

"It's the philosophy of dating," he said.

"Of what?"

"When you meet a boy, you don't want to just sit there and wait for him to make a move on you. You need to be doing something else, so you have a pretext to be together without rushing things. So you go to a movie or something, a shared experience, and that alleviates the awkwardness."

She glanced at him. “Times have changed, Grandpa. We don’t exactly do movies anymore. But maybe you’re right. Shared experience.”

They came to a stream. “That looks very good, along about now,” Llynn said, dismounting. She was breathing hard, and there was a light sheen of sweat on her forehead. Penn knew that the same was true for him. They had been moving well, propelled by the excitement of the chase to they-knew-not-where.

She flopped on the ground and put her mouth to the flowing water. And stopped. “Hey!”

“What?”

“It’s frozen!”

Penn kneeled and touched it with a finger. It was hard, but not chill. “Not exactly. It’s not cold enough.”

She touched it. “You’re right. It’s like plastic.” She looked up at him. “A fake river?”

“Why would anyone bother?” Then he made a connection. “The trees—we can touch them, climb them, smell them, but not affect them. This river’s like that.”

She sat up. “Yeah.” Then she looked at the sky. “Know something else? That sun hasn’t moved since we started, and it’s been at least an hour now.”

Penn looked at his watch, surprised. “Yes. This puts a different complexion on it.”

She got up and stepped on the river. Then she stood on it. “We can’t change things here. But they sure seem real. Can we explain that?”

“This forest,” he said slowly. “If the door is a window to other times, this must be a long time ago. Before there were men to chop down trees. There’s no sign of human presence here. Since man could have come to this continent anywhere up to twenty thousand years ago, that suggests this forest is older. Say thirty thousand years.”

“I’ll buy that. But why can’t we affect it?”

"Because if it's real, it would be paradox. We are in effect visitors from the future. If we change something, we could start a process that results in our not existing."

"Oh, yeah. Like killing your own grandfather." She glanced at him again. "No offense."

"You rub out your grandfather, you're gone," he said with a smile. "I don't think you want to do that."

"For sure. So we can't change anything here. And it's frozen. But why is the sun frozen too? We can't exactly reach up and touch that."

Penn pondered. "Maybe it isn't that there's some temporal law that prevents us from committing paradox. Maybe it's that as visitors we are in a different time frame. So that we are very fleeting, like ghosts."

"Ghosts can walk through walls," she pointed out. "We can't."

Penn continued to work it out. "Suppose our time were a thousand times as fast as the forest time. Then an hour for us would be like a few seconds here. And a minute of its time would like—" he paused, trying to work it out in his head.

"Sixteen hours," she said. "So the sun would hardly move at all. And trees would seem solid, because they're still there no matter how fast we move. And water would flow like frozen molasses. And air—" She paused, startled. "Could we breathe?"

"If we were a thousand times as fast? It would be like a thousand mile an hour hurricane. In fact, I don't think we could move through air that thick."

"But we are moving, and it's not thick at all."

"There goes a good theory," he said ruefully.

Llynn frowned. "It's too good a theory to give up just yet. It accounts for everything except that. We can't make paradox because we're too fleeting. So maybe there's an exception for the air."

"It seems far fetched."

She smiled. "Try it anyway. We've got a good theory to rescue."

"Well, if we are to explore this region at all, or any of the other ones the door accesses, we do have to be able to breathe. Otherwise we die very soon after we step out that door. We have to be able to move, too, without fighting a thousand mile an hour or worse gale. So maybe there is a bubble of air around us—"

"A force field."

"That transfuses oxygen in for us to breathe, and transfuses waste gases out. So we can move and breathe. But it doesn't cover native solids or liquids."

She nodded. "It works for me. Theory saved."

"But it leads to a nervous conjecture. That can't be mere coincidence. Who set this up, to enable us to explore? Who is watching us?"

"Doesn't bother me. The house is a set-up, by something that goes way beyond anything we know. We're guinea pigs. I'm so fascinated that I'm willing to let them watch, for the sake of the weird experience they are giving me. This is better than a super smoke."

"What?" he asked, alarmed.

"I'm joking, Grandpa. I'm not into that stuff. Better than a world class amusement park."

Penn tried to mask his enormous relief. "Do you really feel easy about it?"

"Grandpa, I love the thrill of adventure. That's why I'm dating a bad boy. This is a bigger adventure. Easy? No. Scary? Yes. That's *why* I like it."

He shook his head. "Your grandmother isn't as comfortable about it as you are."

She quickly got serious. "She's not going to quit on the house?"

"I don't think so. But maybe we shouldn't play up the scary aspects."

"For sure. Let's get back before she worries."

They got on the bicycles. Experimentally Llynn rode hers across the surface of the river. Then they headed east, tracking their tree bands.

"The ground's hard," she remarked. "Like the river. The leaves don't crackle under the tires, the sand doesn't give way. That's why it's easy to ride."

"Yes. I also note that there are no animals."

"That's right! They should be standing still. How come we haven't seen any?"

"Maybe there aren't many on the ground, so we just haven't traversed enough territory. But there should be birds."

"How about this: we see birds when they move. If they're frozen in place, we don't notice them. But if we look harder, maybe we will."

"Maybe," he agreed.

Thereafter they scanned the trees and branches as they rode—and soon Llynn did spy a bird. It was just a little wren pecking under a piece of bark, looking like a museum model, but definitely real. Later they spied another bird, flying, hanging in the air between trees.

"Theory confirmed," Llynn said.

They reached the house faster than they had left it, because they were no longer pausing to band trees. They rode up to the boulder in the glade, and the door opened before they stopped. "What a relief!" Chandelle said.

"Something amiss?" Penn asked as they parked the bikes and came to the door.

"Not exactly. I don't feel easy being alone in the house. Little things bother me. Like the plaque."

"The one by the stair that says 1?"

"It said 0 when I first saw it yesterday. This morning it said 1. Now it says 2."

"Some kind of slow clock?" Llynn asked. "Measuring half days?"

"Measuring something," Penn said, leading her to it. Sure enough, the number had changed. "Could be anything. Like how much electricity has been used."

"I'll keep an eye on it," Llynn said. Then, after a pause. "I guess I'd feel nervous, alone in a house like this. Maybe we need another person." She was evidently concerned that Chandelle would decide to leave before all the mysteries were solved.

"Even a pet dog would help," Chandelle said. "It would be aware of things we aren't. They say the very best burglar defense is a dog."

"A dog," Penn mused. "But we may be here only a month. We can't buy a dog just for that. Is there one we could borrow? House trained, friendly, alert?"

"Obsidian," Chandelle said.

"That's cousin Lloyd's dog," Llynn said. "In Okinawa."

"Our son's stationed there now," Penn agreed. "But that's halfway around the world."

"Besides which, Cousin Lloyd is the world's worst brat. Obsidian doesn't go anywhere without him."

Lloyd was thirteen, and mouthy. But if there was one juvenile smarter than Llynn, it was Lloyd. And the idea of the dog had taken hold. "Maybe it would be worth it, to have them both here," Penn said. "Lloyd could figure out the computer, and the dog would guarantee no hostile intrusion."

Llynn glanced at Chandelle. Penn could almost see the girl's thought process: lousy boy, great dog, reassure Grandma. One debit, two credits. "Okay. I guess I can bear that cross for a while. Send them a plane ticket."

"They couldn't get here soon," Chandelle protested. "The dog would have to suffer special handling; she's way too big to carry on board by hand."

"She weighed 87 pounds, last I heard," Penn agreed ruefully. "I guess it was a bad idea."

"No, there must be a way," Llynn said quickly. "Call them, Grandpa. Maybe it would be possible in a couple of days, if there were a family emergency or something."

"Are you suggesting that I pretend—"

"Oh, come on! We're sitting on the weirdest property in the world, right now, and we need to get our dominoes lined up. How do we know what could happen? We need that dog now." Her eyes flicked toward Chandelle. She was facing away from her grandmother, so only Penn saw it, as she intended.

He looked at his wife. "Is there a case?"

"I would feel easier, dear."

There was a case. Chandelle tended to understate things; she was really concerned about the implications of the house. Obsidian would definitely reassure her, and surely be useful in other ways, because she was an extremely curious dog with keen senses. Llynn was eager to stay and fathom the mysteries of the house, which was exactly what they wanted. And Lloyd, obnoxious as he could be at times, was eerily sharp on things the elder generation hardly understood, like computers and the Internet. It seemed like a good team.

Lynne was right: this house and its apertures were strange indeed, and possibly dangerous. They needed their strongest team, and they needed it now.

"I will call," he agreed.

"Great!"

"Thank you dear."

And Penn himself was pleased, because this mystery had galvanized his outlook. He wanted to explore every part of it, as rapidly and competently as possible. It was already clear that there was science here that was unknown to human intellect, and challenges available nowhere else. They had a month to fathom it all, if they could. It promised to be the best month of their lives.

Chapter 3
Llynn

Llynn wasted no time moving into her room. She had thought she would be going home tomorrow, but for once Grandpa had been right: this house was preemptive. And that back yard—that back *world*. What a situation the old folk had found!

At any rate, her folks had delivered her remaining things with alacrity, not inquiring, and she hadn't volunteered. They were afraid she'd change her mind if they said boo, and she was afraid they'd change theirs if they got any whiff of the truth. So it was a conspiracy of silence that suited both parties. Meanwhile, she was glad that the grandparents had discovered this marvelous house, and the truth was, they weren't bad folk at all. She could get along with them. Snotty little Lloyd would be more of a challenge, yet even he would surely see the special nature of this house. He could be trusted to keep his big mouth shut when it was to his advantage, and this definitely was.

She used the toilet, then prettied up at the sink. As she dried her hands, she saw a button in the wall by the bathroom door. One of the especially nice things about this house was that it had a bathroom for every bedroom; no need to share. That meant in turn that she could lock Lloyd out of her room, and that he *couldn't* lock her out of the only bathroom. But there were mysteries galore to fathom yet. What did this button do?

One sure way to find out. She pushed it. There was a swish of sound at the sink. She looked, but the sound stopped before she could identify its source. It had been like water running; she must have left the tap untight.

She looked in the sink. It was bone dry. That was weird. But maybe it was one of the new fangled ceramics that shed water like flowing mercury.

She looked at the button again. So what did it do? The sink had distracted her before she found the answer. So she pushed the button again.

She heard the toilet flushing. She whirled around and got there in one leap. And stared, astonished.

It was flushing backwards.

It really was; the water was swirling around and surging up into its jets. And the—the stuff she had just flushed away—was coming back into the bowl. Was the drainpipe clogged, forcing it to back up? But it had happened only when she pushed the button. Just as the sink had perhaps reversed.

She pushed the button a third time. Nothing happened. But already an answer was coming to her. This button—could it be an Undo feature, like the Oops function on a computer? In which case the reason the third push on it didn't do anything was because there wasn't anything left to undo. She had used the toilet and sink; that was all.

She flushed the toilet again, and there was no problem. Then she washed her hands at the sink again, without trouble. She eyed the button, but decided to leave it alone, this time.

She went downstairs. Grandma was in the kitchen; Grandpa was reading a magazine in the living room. With the TV right there before him, he read a magazine; that was an indication of his generation. But this news might freak the woman out, so she went to the man.

"Grandpa, I discovered something else about this house, I think."

He looked up. "Not dangerous, I trust?"

"It's an undo button. There's one in my bathroom." She looked around. "And there's one here, too." She walked across to indicate the button. "I think it reverses the last thing you did."

"What, make me unread the article I just read?" But he wasn't making fun of it; he looked wary.

"I think it's just what the house does, or what you do with it. Maybe I can test it. I'll turn on the TV; if it turns it off—" She went to the TV set and turned it on.

"But what would be the point?"

"Same as with a computer. Sometimes you make a mistake. This undoes it." She walked to the button. "Ready, Grandpa?" She wasn't sure whether she wanted it to work or to fail.

"Do it," he said.

She pushed the button. The TV turned off.

There was a pause. "Maybe we need a more rigorous test," he said.

"What would be certain?"

"I don't know. What could not happen by chance?"

She pondered. "The back door setting?"

"We tried many settings yesterday, more or lest randomly. Would it reverse them all in turn? That would be persuasive."

They went to the back door. "This is on 6. I tried 5 through 1, so it wasn't really random."

"But perhaps close enough."

There was a button in the wall near the door. She pushed it.

The alien village appeared outside.

They exchanged a glance. Then she pushed the button again. The scene of desolate destruction reappeared. Then, with repeated pushes, the future city, the ugly plain, and the modern city scene.

"That's as far as I went," she said.

"But I experimented before you did," Grandpa said. "I think I remember some of the settings. Here—I'll write them out, and you hold the paper, but don't check until after you push the button."

"Why?"

"So your expectation can't affect the outcome. It's called a single blind experiment." He got paper and pencil and wrote on it, screwing up his forehead to remember. "There; I may not have it all perfect, but it should be close enough to tell." He folded the paper and gave it to her.

Llynn felt a small chill. The real proof was coming. Was that good or bad? She nerved herself and pushed the button.

The forest scene returned. Yes, of course; that was where it had been before she changed the settings. She pushed the button again.

The ugly plain returned. Llynn refrained from looking at the paper, and pushed the button again. The modern city scene showed. She pushed again. Now the scene out back was a new one to her: molten lava.

"I'm going to look now," she said. She opened the paper. He had written PLAIN, CITY, and LAVA. Which was correct, except for the forest, an understandable omission.

"It does seem to be proving out," he said.

"Next is 'Ugly Mountain,'" she said, and pushed the button. A barren rock appeared, with an ugly mountain in the background. "And 'Giant Ferns,'" she read, and pushed it again. The ferns appeared.

"That's as far as I can remember, in order," Penn said. "But there were other scenes. Of different forests."

She pushed the button. Large pine trees appeared. She pushed it once more, and the oak forest was there. "I think that's enough," she said, relieved to see the familiar scene. "I think we have made the case."

"I agree. We do have an Oops button. It may be handy."

They left the back door. As they passed the stair, she looked at the plaque there. Its number was 3. "It changed!" she exclaimed.

"Why so it has," he agreed. "Right after we discovered something new about the house. I wonder whether—"

"It could be an ongoing count of our discoveries," she finished.

And saw the number change to 4.

They both stared. "Llynn, I think we just saw it in action," Penn said. "That plaque marks our progress in learning about this house—and catching on to that was another notch, or milestone, or whatever."

"Which means this house is watching us," she said, feeling a chill again.

He nodded. "So we had better keep alert."

"But what's the point? I mean, why would a house care what we learned about it?"

"That is the sixty four dollar question."

"Grandpa, that figure went out of style decades ago. But do you have an answer?"

"No. But now that I ponder it, I'm not surprised. This house was all set up for us, virtually begging us to rent it. So why shouldn't it keep track of our progress? Maybe it is keeping score."

"And what's the prize when we crack the key number?"

"I wonder. Do you think we're white rats in a maze?"

"Maybe you are. I'm a white mouse."

"Do you think we should get out of this house before we find out?"

She was startled by his directness. "You think it's a honey trap? Get a bunch of us in here, then pickle us as exhibits for posterity?"

"It's a possibility."

Llynn considered. "Why didn't it just do something easy, like having a pile of money on the table? That back door—that's an awful fancy deal just to catch some rodents."

"My thought exactly. This strikes me as more like a training course. Why go to so much trouble, just for a few bodies? So I think we have nothing to lose and perhaps a great deal to gain by pursuing this riddle to its end."

"Right. So what's to pursue next?"

"We have explored the potentials of the back door, but not the front door. It changes too—and maybe it is safe to experiment, considering that we have the Oops button."

"Got it." They headed for the front door.

She peered at the number on its panel. "73. What does that mean?"

"It means that's our present setting. Philadelphia, PA. When I tried the next number up, it was a different city."

"So it's like the back door, with different times?"

"I wonder. Chandelle made me stop experimenting; it made her nervous."

"Why?"

"Because this is the door we need to use to return to our own world. If we interfere with it—"

"Ooo! That makes me nervous too. But you know, Grandpa, we've got the setting. And the Oops button. So we can return to it, same as we did at the back door."

"Yes. Still, it may not be of the same type."

"But that's the challenge, isn't it, Grandpa? To figure it out? So maybe we'd better do that."

He nodded, but his mouth was tight. She knew he felt no easier about this than she did.

She checked for the Oops button, just in case, then moved the number up one to 74.

The scene beyond the window panel changed. "That looks like a different city," she said.

"Yes. But which one?"

"I don't know. Did Philly ever look like this?"

"No. The layout is different."

"So if it's not here in some other time—"

"Could be anywhere."

She saw a car drive by on the street. "American, anyway. Shall we try another?"

"If you wish."

She moved it up to 75. The city changed again. "You recognize this?" she asked.

"No. But American."

"Let's try something different," she said. She set the number at 100. The scone changed.

They stared. "That's Moscow!" Penn exclaimed. "Or some similar Russian city."

She faced him, a revelation growing in her breast. "This isn't time, it's space! Geography. The front door travels across the world."

He turned and walked away.

"Wait, Grandpa! What's the matter?"

"Nothing. I'm just checking the plaque."

She ran after him. "To see if we got it right!"

They looked at the plaque together. Now its number was 5. "We got it right," she breathed, exhilarated.

"Time in back, space in front," he agreed. "This is one versatile house!"

"That gives me a fantastic idea. Can we tune in Okinawa?"

Penn stared at her. "Are you thinking what I think you're thinking?"

"Yeah. Shortcut to pick up the Brat."

They experimented with numbers. The scenes traveled across Asia to Japan. Then they found it: #153. The scene was dark, but the street was lighted. "That's Okinawa," Penn said. "I have been there."

Llynn's chill remained, but there was gladness in it. "So can we just go and fetch him in?"

"That would suggest that we have instant travel. Teleportation. That's hard to believe."

"So's this whole house, Grandpa."

"Let me check with Chandelle."

This made Llynn nervous in another way. "What if she vetoes it?"

"Then maybe she's right."

"Yeah, maybe."

But Chandelle didn't object. "Do what you have to do," she said. "But be careful."

"We'll go," Penn decided. "But not right now. Better do it by daylight."

"What time is it over there, now?" Llynn asked, peering out.

"Well, it's about noon here, and they run about ten hours earlier."

"Earlier? But they're west, where they lag behind us."

Penn smiled in the knowledgeable manner of his generation. "Precisely. Then sun rises later there, if we ignore the effect of the international Date Line. So the hour seems earlier. So over there, the time should be about two AM."

"Oh." Lynn got the logic of it straight in her mind. "I guess they wouldn't like us paying a call right now."

"I guess not," he agreed. "So why don't we wait until six PM, our time, which will be 8 AM their time? They should be up and about then."

"And maybe we'd better take a nap, or something, to avoid jet lag, or whatever."

"Or whatever," he agreed equably.

They had lunch, and Llynn went to her room to sleep. She seldom slept during daytime, but could do it when she had to. There was a small TV in her room, with an amazing array of channels; she put it on something dopey, and managed to drift in and out for a couple of hours.

Toward six by her watch she roused herself, put on clean jeans—her size was in the closet, interestingly, so she really hadn't needed her own clothing—and went down to find Penn. It was now light outside the house. She reminded herself that it was morning here in the far Pacific, not late afternoon.

"Do be careful," Grandma Chandelle said, in her grandmotherly way.

The two of them got in the car. The garage door rolled itself up, and they backed out. Penn drove carefully along the unfamiliar streets. "It has been a while since I've been here," he said. "But I know the address." He glanced at her. "There's just one question. Assuming that we find them—"

"How do we explain how we got here so fast?" she finished. "Maybe I better handle that, Grandpa. I'm better at lying."

"This is not a trait we encourage in you."

"This is necessary, isn't it? We need something persuasive, because we can't let the truth out."

He nodded. She knew he didn't like it, but was up against a wall. "You may have a point. Very well, you handle it. I will wait in the car. Assuming—"

"Assuming it's real, and not just another still picture." But they had seen other moving cars. "I've got my weirdness censor turned off right now. But maybe I'll scream in the night, when the rest of it hits me."

"Don't scream. Just come to us. I don't want to think you've been eaten by an alien monster."

"It's a deal." They were halfway bantering, but they both were nervous.

"This seems to be the address," he said, pulling up to a house.

"Oh? I thought they'd be in a barracks or something."

"Not the married, familied ones, with time in the service. They live offpost."

"Okay." She opened the door and got out. "Here goes—whatever."

"If you have any misapprehension—"

"I'll get back here in a hurry," she agreed.

She was not as easy about this as she pretended. Could they really be in Okinawa, just by the turn of a knob? No feeling of motion, no nothing? Could this be a movie set, and behind that door would be something incredibly weird? She nerved herself and marched down the walk.

She reached the door, nerved herself again, and knocked. She was in luck: the boy answered. "Cousin Snoot!" he exclaimed, using one of his insulting names for her. "You here already?"

"We caught a fast flight, cousin Brat," she responded. "You

ready to go?"

"Why the hoohaw would I want to go anywhere with you, Cousin Bitchy?"

It was certainly him. She controlled her irritation. "Well, we don't need you. Just let us have Obsidian."

"No way, Snootay!"

She didn't have much time to make an impression. In a moment an adult would appear. "Lloyd, I've go a deal for you. Come see our house. If you don't like it, you're free to go home."

"From the Yoo Ess Ay? Fatty chance."

"Our house *here*. You can be there and back here within an hour. Deal?"

"I don't have to do that much, Cous. I like it right here."

"Lloyd, take my word, for once: there is something you will want to see. In the back yard. I'll show you. Then—"

"If you're going to show me your titties, forget it. I'm your *cousin*."

He was trying to get her goat, and succeeding. But she refused to give him the satisfaction. "Not that, you little peeper. Something you never dreamed of. But I'll make you this deal: if you aren't satisfied with what you see there, I'll pay a penalty: I *will* show you my breasts."

That scored. Lloyd, like all thirteen year old brats, had a deep fascination with the forbidden; that was why he derided it. "Really? And you won't tell?"

She nodded, and extended her hand. "Deal?"

He touched her finger through the screen. "Deal!"

"Then check with your folks. Grandpa Penn is out front in the car."

"No need. I'm home alone for the day." He turned. "Obsidian!"

The huge dog bounded up behind him, tail wagging. He put the leash on her, and stepped out the door. Obsidian eagerly sniffed Llynn, remembering her.

"She looks even bigger than before," Llynn said.

"Ninety six and a half pounds," Lloyd said proudly. "And no fat. Come on." He and the dog forged down the walk.

Soon they were in the car. "Lloyd's folks are already off at the post," Llynn said. "I made him a deal: he can go right back home if he doesn't like our back yard."

"Yeah," the boy agreed, sending her a sharp glance. Of course they would not tell the old folk of the other part of their deal.

Penn drove carefully back the way they had come. Obsidian sniffed every smell that wafted in the cracked-open window. She loved any ride in any car, anywhere, except maybe to the vet.

They arrived, and parked in the garage. "This way," Llynn said, leading boy and dog to the back door. Penn stayed clear, knowing what was coming.

"Here, maybe I'd better take the dog," Llynn said as they came to the door.

Lloyd looked at her suspiciously, but handed over the leash. With her free hand, Llynn opened the door and let him out.

Then she had to hang on for dear life, as the huge dog charged out after him, tail wagging. Obsidian weighed almost as much as she did, and was not properly leash trained; Llynn was hauled along toward the nearest tree.

"So it's a forest," Lloyd said derisively. "So what?"

"Turn around," she told him on the way by.

He turned. "Say! Where's the house?"

"Who knows!" she called mischievously.

"What's it, a mirror or something?"

"Must be," she agreed as the dog came to the tree.

Lloyd walked back to the boulder, trying to figure it out. She let him stew. She wanted to make him come to her for the answer. So she watched as he touched the boulder, verifying its reality. As he climbed on it. As he looked beyond it. As he shook his head.

"Okay, I give up," he called. "What gives?"

"It's an endless forest," she said. "Grandpa and I explored it, but never found the end. It's frozen, too; nothing moves. And it's only the beginning."

"Show me."

She tugged at the leash. "Come on, Obsidian; we've got business." The dog, eager to get to new things, came readily along.

She went to where she knew the door was, and knocked on the boulder. It opened immediately, and Penn showed in the opening. He had of course been waiting for this.

"Wow!" Lloyd exclaimed. "I gotta check this out." He dashed in, and disappeared in the house.

Llynn and Obsidian followed. The boy ran through the house and out the front door. She knew what he would find: a house surrounded by city.

In a moment Lloyd came back. He went out the back door. Then back inside. "Only the beginning?"

Llynn smiled. "Watch this." She punched #1 on the back door panel. The alien village appeared. "But I wouldn't go out there just yet. We don't know whether they eat people."

He stared. "How'd you find this place? There's nothing like this on Okinawa."

"We brought it with us from America."

"Oh, yeah?" he was still looking for the catch.

"I'll show you." She led the way to the front door, and put #73 on the panel. Philadelphia appeared.

"That's America!" Lloyd said. "And it's evening!"

"It's halfway around the world," Llynn agreed. "The sun's on the other side."

Lloyd went out the front door again. He sniffed the air and scuffed his sole on the pavement. Then he returned to the house. "Okay, you got me. I'll stay. But you gotta show me how you do it."

"To the extent we are able," Penn said. "We have learned a little about this house, and know that the back door opens on time, and the front on space. But how it is accomplished, and why it is offered here for us, we have no inkling. We are hoping that you will help us solve the riddle of it all."

"The TV's something special too," Llynn said. "All channels, and the Internet."

Lloyd eyed the TV. "*All* channels?"

Penn caught her eye. She got the hint. "Well, we're not sure," she said diplomatically. "We figured you'd be better at figuring it out. Especially the alien stations."

The boy paused. "Like the front door, back door?"

"We think so," she agreed.

"Okay, like I said, I'm in. I'll get my things. But what do I tell my folks?"

Penn exited the room, tacitly giving Llynn leave to handle it her way. She did. "You know we can't tell them the truth. We can't tell anyone, outside of us. It's not just because they wouldn't believe it."

"They'd freak out," he said seriously. "They'd never let me go. So what's the cover story?"

"We took a fast flight to Okinawa, and have a fast flight back. You're with us for a month, and we'll return you then. We've got a real nice place, and plenty of ice cream, and Obsidian loves it."

He shook his head. "Girls and old folk are no good at lying. My folk's'll check the flight schedules, and want to know why I'm suddenly getting along with you."

He had a point. He *was* better at lying. "You have a way to handle it?"

"First, I'll go online and fake up a flight schedule and bookings that'll fool them."

"You can do that?" she asked, letting her awe show.

"Sure. Provided Grandpa lets me fool with his bank account, so the tickets are paid for. Later I'll cancel, so he's not out the money, but for now it's better to keep that aspect straight. My folk won't check again later; why should they? And if they did, they'd figure the cancellation is a misprint, since obviously I did take the flight with you folk."

She nodded. "I'll talk to Grandpa. He'll do it. What about the other?"

"I'm not sure. We're going to be fighting. I know it, you know it, the world knows it. I could visit with the old folk, sure, but it'd take a miracle to make me do it the same time as you."

"And we don't want them to catch on to the nature of that miracle."

Lloyd paced the floor. "You know, you won, so you don't have to show me your—you know. But you know—"

"If your folks thought I'd show you anything, they'd ground you before you could blink."

"Yeah. And I'm not trying to renege on that, though if I ever get the chance to peek, you know I will. But what I'm thinking is, well, I'm thirteen, and kids my age are starting to date, and—"

"And for all your cleverness on the Net, you don't know beans about girls," she finished.

"Yeah. And it's rough. So if—"

"Are you asking for a course in dating?"

Lloyd fidgeted. "I guess I am."

"You got it. You'll be a perfect gentleman when you return."

"Yeah." He tried to look glum, but it was evident his heart wasn't in it. It was a perfect excuse, and probably he really did want to learn the social ropes, so as not to be clumsy when the time came.

"Good enough," she said. "Let's do it."

Then Lloyd paused. "Oops. I just thought of something."

She had a notion what. "That again? Okay, just this once, and don't tell." She hooked her fingers into her shirt and drew it up, flashing him with her bra. Then, quickly, she tucked her shirt back into her waistband.

He looked as if he had just been given a view of heaven and hell. "Uh, thanks. But you didn't have to do that. What I meant was Obsidian. She can't ride with us on a commercial flight."

Oops. Well, it had been fun flashing him, regardless. "But she won't have to. She—" Then Llynn caught his point. "Special arrangements for a dog. Animals can't travel the way people do. There are quarantines, delays—that's tough." Then it came to her. "Since this isn't really happening, we don't care how awkward it is. All we need is a manifest or something accounting for the dog. You can do that online. Ship her by herself, and we'll take her to the right office. On our own. We say."

He brightened. "Got it. I can do it now. Where's the terminal?"

"This way." She led him to the den with the computer.

He turned it on. The screen lighted, PLEASE SELECT DESIRED OPTION. There was a list of programs. "Wow! You weren't just kidding about what this has. Windows, DOS, CP/M, UNIX, OS/2, and stuff I haven't even heard of." He typed choices and codes, and the screen changed. "And look at the system specs! I didn't know they made power or speed like this."

"They don't, I think," Llynn said. "It's this house."

"I like this house! And look at the online services—it's got them all, first class and paid for. I don't even have to hack in. And browsers galore, versions from the future, maybe. I feel like I just stepped from a propeller plane to an interplanetary rocket." He was already online, moving with a sureness she could only envy.

"Probably you did, in terms of computing."

"Yeah. This is like changing numbers on the doors: there's a fantastic universe here. I think some of it really *is* alien, but set up to be simple to use." He glanced up at her. "You know, you—I mean, thanks for what you showed me. The flash. But this is more interesting, no insult. I could get lost in this."

"The time will come when a woman does similar to you. When she's not your cousin."

"Maybe. Okay, stop bugging me and let me at this. I got miles to go before I sleep."

"Robert Frost," she said, naming the poet he had inadvertently quoted. But he was already lost in the wonders of the system. She repressed her irritation and departed.

Penn was waiting. “He’s online, setting it up,” she said. “Phantom tickets on flights for us, and shipping for Obsidian, to America. I told him you’d let him tap into your bank account to pay for the tickets; he’ll cancel the charges after his folks verify them.”

“Virtual paper trail,” Penn agreed. “I won’t inquire about the details.”

“Right. Let us juvenile delinquents do the talking.” She looked around. “Where is Obsidian?”

“Chandelle’s taking her for a walk out back. I wish I knew exactly what she’s sniffing.”

“You know, Grandpa, I do feel better for having the dog along. And Lloyd—our cover story is that I’ll teach him social etiquette, for when he starts dating. But I guess I’m glad to have him along too, bratty as he is. He really does know the Internet.”

“I’m glad to hear it. I’ll reset the house for Okinawa.”

“Okay, but we’re not ready to go out yet. Lloyd’s still handling things online.”

“And Chandelle’s still out exploring.” He paused contemplatively. “This is the first time she has been out back on her own. Obsidian really gives her confidence.”

“Gives us all confidence,” she agreed. “Say—if you changed the front door setting while someone was out back, would it mess them up? I mean, like lost in time?”

Penn actually sat down in a chair, looking quite sober. “I hadn’t thought of that. The settings seem to have been constant, one not affecting the other, but I think I would not care to risk having any of us outside when we made a change of any kind. Perhaps we should establish a policy to that effect. Just in case.”

“Just in case,” she echoed, feeling a chill.

“So I will not reset the front door yet. And we perhaps should have all of us assembled before we make any future changes.

Otherwise someone might change the back setting while another was out there."

"And I've got a feeling that there's nothing so lost, as lost in time," Llynn said, her chill much worse. "All five of us in sight before anyone touches a panel. In fact—" She paused, working it out. "In fact, maybe you should be the only one to touch those panels, Grandpa. So there's never any question."

"Perhaps so. I can ask the others. Perhaps each member of the group should have a particular responsibility, upon which the others will not infringe without specific permission. An area of expertise, so to speak."

"Yes. Because we don't know what we're into, really. We need to cover our bases, just in case."

Lloyd entered the living room. "Okay, it's done. Let's go get my stuff." He headed for the front door.

"No!" Penn and Llynn said together.

Lloyd stopped moving. "Something I should know?"

Llynn explained about their policy, and that Chandelle was out back with the dog. Lloyd nodded. "Okay by me. Can I have the computer?"

Llynn exchanged a glance with Penn. "Very well," Penn said. "The computer is yours. Just don't run my account broke. What about you, Llynn?"

"I'll take the TV. That's got some weird stuff."

"Very well," Penn repeated. "I suspect Chandelle will want the kitchen and household appliances."

"Isn't she about due back?" Llynn inquired, suppressing another infiltration of nervousness.

"Yes." Penn got up and walked to the back. Llynn and Lloyd followed.

The woman and dog were just coming into sight from the forest. Relieved, they opened the door for her. "It's marvelous, but so eerie," Chandelle said, out of breath. "Nothing moves. But Obsidian loves it."

"It surely is best that she be acquainted with the surrounding region," Penn said. "So she will know immediately if there is any intrusion."

"Yes, she's so alert," Chandelle agreed. It was clear that the presence of the dog was transforming her concern about the premises.

They caught Chandelle up on their idea of responsibilities, and on Lloyd's online arrangements. She agreed. "Now let's get Lloyd settled, and Obsidian, of course." She glanced at Lloyd. "Will she mind remaining with me when you go out?"

"Not if I tell her it's okay," the boy said. "She knows you, Grandma. But anybody new, we'll have to be careful."

"That suits me exactly," Chandelle said.

Penn, in the presence of the others, reset the front door. It had been darkening into dusk out front; suddenly it was bright daylight. Then Penn and Llynn went with Lloyd in the car, while Obsidian remained in the house with Chandelle. They were, as it were, on their way.

Chapter 4
Lloyd

It wasn't any breeze, but Lloyd managed to convince his parents that it was okay for him and Obsidian to go immediately to America with the grandparents and his cousin. After all, the old folk had the arrangements all made, and had to return immediately or face complications. When his mother was suspicious, knowing how he usually fought with Llynn, he scuffed his toes and admitted that the girl had promised to teach him how to be a social gentleman. That impressed Mom; she'd been trying to make him social for years. Dad just looked away, maybe suspecting that Lloyd was entering the age when his interest in girls changed from indifferent to attentive. The fact was, Llynn *was* becoming attractive, with her long glossy black hair and slender but not exactly thin figure. But it wasn't his business to notice that; he was indeed her cousin. Almost, he regretted that.

So they went back to the house, with more of Lloyd's things than he really needed, considering all the stuff the house had. In his size, too. But he hadn't been able to tell his folks about that, of course. So he stashed his stuff in his room, with Grandpa's help, while Grandma saw about fixing them a snack. Grandma was good that way. Obsidian found the whole business fascinating, and was constantly racing around the house to keep up with what everyone was doing.

"I think that dog's philosophy of life," Penn remarked, "is that there is nothing in the world that can't be improved by the addition of a cold wet nose."

"Yeah."

There was a scream. Alarmed, they ran to the living room, arriving there just after Chandelle.

It was Llynn, and she was furious. She had changed into a short skirt, and Obsidian was standing near, looking at her with perplexity.

"What happened?" Chandelle asked.

"That dog! She goosed me with her nose!"

Suddenly Lloyd caught on. Obsidian wasn't supposed to sniff crotches, but sometimes when excited she still did it. That short skirt had been too much of a temptation.

Lloyd tried to keep a straight face, but the mental image of the dog adding her cold wet nose to what was under the skirt got to him, and he started laughing helplessly. Llynn glared at him, but that just made it worse.

"I'll put Obsidian in our bedroom for now," Chandelle said, evidently fearing an explosion. She called to the dog, and the two of them departed.

"You just gotta tell her no," Lloyd managed to say as Llynn stalked off to her own room. He stifled another eruption of laughter.

Penn changed the front door, and just like that they were back in America.

The time was different. It was night here. The other three were on Eastern Standard Time, so had no problem, but Lloyd was on Okinawa time. He wasn't nearly ready to turn in.

"No problem," Penn said. "You stay up and explore the computer while we sleep. We'll get in phase in time."

So Lloyd did. But though the Internet was fascinating—he had not had completely free access to it before—he became increasingly conscious that he was alone, at least in terms of being awake. He wasn't used to that. So he got up and went into the living room.

Llynn appeared, in her baby doll pajamas and bathrobe. "What's with you?" she asked.

"Not ready to sleep, not ready to be alone," he said honestly. "Look, about what Obsidian did—"

"Not your fault. Forget it."

Which meant she preferred to bury the incident. "Okay. Look, I don't want to keep you up if you're sleepy, but this house is weird. I—do you wanna play a computer game or something?"

She smiled. "Okay, I had a nap in the afternoon, so I don't need a full night's sleep. How about a dating lesson?"

"Okay." He had not been serious about that, but as company she was better than nothing, and it was something to do.

"So here you are, at a school dance," she said. "Have you any idea how to proceed?"

"Depends on the step."

"Let's make it an old fashioned waltz, the kind the grandfolk like."

"I hate that kind."

"Which is why you had better learn it, so you'll never be embarrassed. It would be just your luck to encounter a girl who knew only that. Here's the step; come on and try it." She demonstrated with her feet.

"Yeah, I've seen it. I know the step. Only—"

"Do you? Try it with me." She held out her arms, and he had to step into her embrace or balk.

So he stepped in. "Hold me here and here," she said, setting his arms in place. "Do *not* let your right hand drop low, if you ever want to dance with that girl again. But you can hold her reasonably snug."

They got into the step, at first not well coordinated, but then better. He wouldn't care to tell her, but she was actually a pretty nice armful. They were the same height, as he still had some growing to do, but her body was dramatically different, by touch. If he closed his eyes and pretended she wasn't his cousin, he could get to like her.

"No," she said. "You're following me. You're supposed to lead."

"Lead?"

"Like this." She assumed a straighter stance, and began moving him around. "You're the hard man; I'm the soft woman."

"Hey, stop shoving!" he protested, shoving back.

"Not like that," she said. "Like this." She pushed him again.

"Like hell!" He wrapped his arms around her and jammed her against the wall.

"What are you doing?" she demanded, glaring into his face from close range.

"I don't like getting pushed around." He jammed her harder.

"Why you stupid little snot!" she exclaimed. Then she put her arms around him, heaved him up off his feet, and tried to throw him down. But he was holding onto her too tightly, and they both fell twisting to the floor.

"So you want to fight, you bitch," he panted, and tried to wrestle her around under him.

"You started it, you idiot," she panted back. She shoved him part-way away from her, and held him down with one bare knee over his legs. She was trying to get her hands free, and he realized that her sharp nails could do some real damage. So he hung on to her wrists and tried to throw her off.

Lloyd discovered, in the course of the struggle, that she was as strong as he, and she was no shrinking violet. For all her talk about being a soft woman, she was a lean female panther, not giving way in any respect. He wished he hadn't gotten into this.

"What's going on here?" It was Penn, with Chandelle right behind him.

Disaster! They fell apart and scrambled to their feet. Lloyd's clothing was okay, but Llynn's bathrobe and pajamas were sadly askew. The robe was open, and her baby dolls were twisted and pulled up so that she was showing more limb and torso than any grandparents would approve. She quickly put herself back together, but this would be tough to explain to the elders.

"Did he attack you?" Penn demanded of Llynn, and his usually amiable face was frighteningly serious.

Lloyd suddenly realized that he could be in real trouble. If

Llynn even hinted that he had tried to molest her, he would be doomed; they'd never believe him.

Llynn laughed. "No, of course not! I was—once I was out alone on the street, and there was this man, and I was afraid he was going to come after me. He didn't, but it scared me. So I asked Lloyd to show me what to do if a man got me down, and he said to use my knee. But I wasn't sure it would work. So we agreed that if I could knee him in the—the stomach, that would make the point. In real life. I wasn't trying to do it hard. But you know, it's not easy to make it work without practice. I still don't have it right."

Penn considered. "Well, next time warn us before you practice. And don't do it in nightclothes."

"Come, dear," Chantelle said, taking Llynn by the arm. "Let's have some hot chocolate." They went to the kitchen.

"Guess I'm better turn in," Lloyd said, realizing that his cousin had covered for him. That amazed him, but he was not about to throw away the alibi.

"Let's wait a moment," Penn said, and there was nothing in his tone that brooked any resistance. "We have to talk."

"Uh, sure." Lloyd did not like the smell of this.

"What really happened?"

So the grandparents hadn't bought it. Chandelle was probably questioning Llynn similarly in the kitchen. If their stories didn't match—

So he told the truth. "It was the other way around. She was teaching me to dance, and I messed up." He went on to give the details.

"Well, I think you owe her one," Penn said at last.

"Yeah," Lloyd agreed fervently.

"And if there's ever another fight in this house, you had better be defending her."

"Yeah."

"Now I think you had better turn in."

"Yeah." It was a dismissal that reminded him that Grandpa, like Dad, was an old military man. Lloyd had been put on notice, and there would be no recourse if he ever messed up similarly again.

Lloyd went to the den and shut down the system. Then he went to his room. He took a shower, donned his pajamas, and lay down on the bed. He wasn't sleepy, but there was nothing else to do.

He knew he had been wrong throughout. Llynn had been trying to show him how to lead, and he had reacted as if she were attacking him. As if she had been a boy pushing him around. In retrospect, he saw his actions as crazy. He *had* started it, pointlessly, making an utter fool of himself. By letting his automatic reflexes govern him, when they were not appropriate. By being the damned brat his cousin thought he was.

Yet Llynn had tried to cover for him. She could have gotten him in real trouble, and instead had lied to spare him. That shook him up as much as his bad reactions did. Why had she done it?

For a long time he pondered that, working it out. She wanted him to help figure out the house. They wanted the dog, too. He understood that. But mainly, it was that she understood him well enough to know that he hadn't been in control. That he had acted like the mouthy juvenile he was. And she wasn't going to make it any worse for him than that. That was an aspect of decency in her he hadn't seen before.

He did owe her. Meanwhile, he had better grow up, so that he never again embarrassed himself that way.

Then, at last, he slept.

Next day no one spoke of the episode. Instead they encouraged him to explore the limits of the computer system. Did it offer any hint of the nature or purpose of the house? And he had to admit that if it did, he was as yet unable to fathom it. There were indeed what seemed to be alien connections, but they answered to codes he had not yet figured out. Their security was good; he could not get past their fire-walls.

Chandelle went out shopping, and Penn took Obsidian and went for a walk in the forest. Lloyd took advantage of the opportunity to talk to Llynn alone. She was in the living room watching the TV, trying new channels. She looked up as he entered, not speaking.

"Look," he said awkwardly. "I'm not good at this. I—I messed up yesterday, and I'm sorry. I—"

"Are you apologizing?" she asked.

"Yeah. Trying to. I got—it's just that when somebody pushes me—I—I guess I—"

"Okay. Apology accepted."

"Yeah. Thanks. But why did you try to cover for me?"

"I knew you didn't mean it, Lloyd. And I thought they wouldn't believe what actually happened. No point in getting you in trouble for nothing."

He nodded. "I guess you are more mature than I am. But thanks. And if you—I really do want to learn to dance—but after what I did—"

She smiled. "I'll teach you. I promised to have you civilized in a month. So don't make a liar out of me."

"I won't. But I think I owe you." He looked at the TV, wanting a way to leave this subject behind. "Found anything interesting?"

She looked around, making sure Penn wasn't back. "Maybe. Maybe I should get your input."

"My input?"

"On this." She touched the remote control, and a new station appeared. It showed a handsome young man, and a well endowed young woman, embracing. Both were naked.

Lloyd stared. "That's porno!"

"I think so. I haven't seen much of it. Have you?"

"Not a lot," he said guardedly. He looked more closely. "Not this good."

"I'm curious. That position they're assuming—do real people actually do that?"

"Maybe if they're athletic. God, that's hot!"

"That turns a man on?"

"Just the sight of a naked woman turns a man on—and she's the shapeliest, sexiest one I've ever seen. Ever even imagined."

"I'm looking at the man. The—what they're doing doesn't exactly turn me on, but he's some hunk. Are they really—really endowed like that?"

He laughed. "Sure. Just like all women have boobs like hers."

"Which means hardly any do."

"Yeah. But what a show to watch!"

"Is this really what all men would be doing, if they had the chance?"

"Oh, yeah! If they had the chance. With a babe like that."

"That's interesting." She was affecting disinterest, but she was watching as closely as he was. He realized that girls weren't supposed to have any sexual interest, but maybe they did, some.

They lapsed into silence, watching.

After a time he heard Llynn's sharp intake of breath, and glanced at her—and saw Penn standing in the doorway. He had returned, and they had been so wrapped up in the show that they hadn't noticed. How were they going to get out of this?

Penn walked to another chair and sat down, watching the show. He didn't say a word.

The two of them sat frozen, unable to figure out a thing to say or do. Lloyd glanced sidelong at Llynn. She looked as if about to faint.

Then Chandelle entered the room. He hadn't heard the car return. She took another chair and sat down, silently. Worse yet!

Finally Lloyd nerved himself for action. He stood, walked to the set, and turned it off. "I shouldn't have put this on," he said. "I'm sorry."

Penn and Chantelle got up and left the room. Llynn recovered. There were red dabs of color on her cheeks. "I think you just paid me back," she said.

"Glad to." As a bratty boy, he could be expected to get into mischief like this. As an innocent young lady, she wasn't. So he had covered for her.

So it was they reached their accommodation. They did after all have more in common than they did with the elder generation. But what unified them all was this fantastic house and its associated mysteries.

Lloyd returned to the computer, exploring its by-paths. He could reach anywhere in the world, talk with anyone, learn anything, except what he most wanted: what was the secret of this house? Who had built it, and why was it being offered free for a month to Penn and Chandelle? Llynn had shown him the plaque at the foot of the stairs, that she said clicked over to a new number every time they discovered something significant about the house. He wanted to make such a discovery, and have a number click for him. But there was no information about this house anywhere on the Internet. He knew, because he had tried a search with three truly powerful search engines. This house did not exist, as far as the world was concerned. Somehow that wasn't surprising, but it was frustrating.

They had meals, and discussed things, and he took Obsidian out for a walk in the forest. She loved it, but he didn't dare let her run loose, because how would they find her if she got lost? They still didn't know what might be out there. Maybe not a bear or saber toothed cat, but what about a deadly tar pit or sink hole that would swallow her up forever?

Penn and Llynn experimented with the front door settings, making a list, trying to catalogue them by location. There seemed to be an endless number of preset cities, ranging from tropical to arctic. Who had zeroed them in and assigned the numbers? That must be one of the mysteries they had to fathom.

Lloyd was tired by evening, but couldn't yet sleep. Jet lag, for all that he hadn't taken any jet; it just took time to acclimatize. He watched a movie on the TV with the others, then tried to turn in, but it was no go. Obsidian was restless too, but he didn't care to go out with her by night, for all that it wasn't necessarily night out back. The others were asleep, and they had agreed not to leave the house alone without checking with Chandelle first. It was a good rule; if he went out and then couldn't find the door, what then? There was just too much they didn't yet know about this place.

He turned on the room TV he had. There was another movie on, with a pretty girl who reminded him a little of Llynn. He thought about the fight he had had with Llynn, ashamed for what he had done. She was a *girl*; boys weren't supposed to fight with girls. Whatever had possessed him? She had been so feminine; there was no way to mistake her for a boy who might be pushing him around.

Then it came to him: he had reacted *because* she was feminine. He hadn't wanted to admit that he was attracted to her. She was his cousin, a creature of contempt. So he had rejected her, turning his disgust with himself into something else. Once he had done the first push, the rest had followed.

Somehow the realization didn't make him feel better. He had been a jerk, whatever the reason. But maybe now he would be less of a jerk. Certainly he would try.

Obsidian whined and pawed at the bedroom door. "We can't go out now," he told her. But she still nosed the doorknob, asking. "Okay, just in the house," he said. He didn't need the leash for that.

He though she would want to go downstairs, but she stopped in the hall, sniffing the air, floor, and walls. "What is it?" he asked, though of course she couldn't answer.

Her attention centered on a spot in the center of the hall about equidistant from the three bedrooms. There was nothing on the floor; he checked. No rug, no trapdoor, no nothing, just floor. Yet obviously she smelled something, and he knew from long experience that there was always reason for her interest, however subtle it might be.

So he cast about. The floor seemed tight, but there could be a switch that slid a panel aside to reveal a secret compartment or did something else. Maybe there was a stair to an attic. The house had a basement with a furnace, but no attic. If there was an attic that they hadn't found, this might be where to find the access to it.

He inspected the walls carefully, looking for any smudge that might betray a panel. There was none. But he did find a hole in the wall. It was weird, because it wasn't visible, but his hand felt it. In fact the tips of his fingers disappeared into it. A recessed panel, covered by a holographic illusion of wall. Now he was getting somewhere.

He felt a button on that panel, so he pressed it. And something fascinating happened.

There was a faint swirl of color in the center of the hall, right where Obsidian had been so avidly sniffing. It thickened, forming the outline of a staircase. But it wasn't real. He put his hand through it. A holographic stair!

That put him in mind of a poem he had heard. Something about yesterday upon the stair, seeing a man who wasn't there. Only in this case it was the stair that wasn't there. But what good was it, if it couldn't be used?

The stairway clarified, until it was completely opaque and looked quite real. But it had no substance. He could walk right through it. He did so, twice, keeping his eyes open. There was a moment of misty darkness while his head was in it, then the other side.

Now he knew what Obsidian had been looking for. The dog saw it too; she put her nose in it and sniffed, but evidently it had no smell. Holographs didn't, because they weren't really there.

However, there must be something there, because otherwise she wouldn't have been aware of it at all. Maybe an invisible energy pattern.

Lloyd pondered. This house wasn't given to pretense; it had things that the world had never seen elsewhere. So there had to be substance to this illusion. He just had to figure out how to find it.

Well, suppose it was what it looked like: a stairway to an attic? But suppose it needed to be out of the way most of the time? Just like regular attic stairs, that pulled down from the ceiling, and you wouldn't even know they were there if you didn't see the outline of crevices in the ceiling, and pull on the string to bring the stairs down? So naturally this house couldn't do it the old fashioned way; it had a holographic stair. But maybe that just marked the place, so you could walk through it carrying your junk, then solidify it when you were ready to ascend? There must be another button to do that. Or maybe the same button, again. Like a double click on the computer, to do more than the single click.

He put his finger in the hidden panel, found the button, and pushed it again. There was a moderately clear click, and a ridge of light appeared along the staircase. Cautiously Lloyd touched it—and it was solid. He had done it!

He put his foot on the lowest step. It remained solid. Would the house let him get halfway up, then make it misty again so he would fall? He didn't think so, but he wasn't sure he should chance it. Probably he should wait until morning and tell the others, and they could all work it out together.

Then Obsidian, ever-eager, lurched by him and scrambled up the stairs to disappear into the ceiling. So much for waiting. Lloyd hurried up after her. When his head reached the ceiling, it passed through it; the stairs were solid while the ceiling wasn't, in this section. Beyond it was a lighted attic, with sloping ceiling panels.

Lloyd stepped off the stair, then paused. Suppose somebody came along and pushed the button again, turning it off, or making it back into a holograph, so that when he stepped on it he fell to the floor? There had to be a button up here, just in case.

He looked around, seeing nothing. So he felt around, and found another invisible recessed panel in the ceiling nearest the stair, and pushed it. The lights went out, and sure enough, the stair was gone. He pushed the button again, and lights and stair returned. Now he had it.

Obsidian was sitting nearby, waiting for him to do something interesting. "You found it," he told her. "You knew about the stairs. But what's up here?"

He looked around the attic. There was a walkway along the center line, and on either side were marked squares with objects sitting in them. None of the objects were familiar. Some were like boxes, and some like cloth, but only approximately; they were clearly alien artifacts. What were they, and what were they doing here? If they were for the residents of the house to use, why were they hidden up here? If they weren't, why were they here at all, with a special stairway for access?

Then he had a bright notion: these things were one of the challenges of the house. Something for the people to find. When they were ready.

Well, he wouldn't touch the things now. This was something for the whole family to explore. He did think of the four of them as a family, now, united by their experience with this house. And maybe he had just contributed his part to their joint effort.

"Come, on, Obsidian," he said. The dog scrambled down the stairs head first, and Lloyd followed more carefully. He found the panel and button below, and pushed, and the stairs faded into translucency and then to nothing.

He went downstairs and looked at the plaque. Sure enough: the number had changed to 6. He had made his mark.

He returned to his bedroom, where the TV was still on. He

turned it off, took a shower, put on his pajamas, and lay down on his bed. He thought he would be wide awake, thinking about his discovery, but this time he dropped off to sleep.

Chapter 5
Obsidian

Chandelle got up before Penn and went down to the kitchen to start breakfast and the day, as she usually did. She had always been a "late" person, retiring after midnight and waking after eight AM, but since coming to this house she had become an "early" person. Maybe she would revert once she got used to it.

She went to the front door, and there was the newspaper. She wondered whether it would be a Chinese newspaper if the door were set on a Chinese city overnight; they might have to try that sometime. She brought it in, and Obsidian bounded up, seeking attention. She welcomed the dog, rubbing her ears and patting her solid shoulder; she really did feel more comfortable with an alert dog in the house.

But had Obsidian been outside yet? Better not to risk it. She put the leash on and they went out back to explore the forest. The trees might be like statues, but they did look nice, and it was a truly peaceful scene.

The dog strained at the leash, pulling this way and that, not trying to escape so much as eager to smell every single possible thing in the area. Then she went to a brushy place and did her business. They would have to take a longer walk sometime, or maybe explore one of the other settings; most of the settings seemed safe enough, and even the lava one wasn't actually hot. But so far she hadn't convinced herself that it was safe to walk on flowing volcanic rock.

But now there was breakfast to make, so they couldn't stay out. It was nice, in its fashion, to have the feel of a family again; she had forgotten the busy-ness of it. Chandelle tugged on the leash, and the dog headed for the house just as eagerly.

There was of course no sign of the house, because it disappeared when the door closed. There was only the boulder. But Chandelle had marked the spot where the door was, and Obsidian was able to sniff it out unerringly anyway. As they approached the door, it opened: Lloyd was there.

"Grandma! I found something," the boy said. "And the number clicked over."

That meant it was significant. "What is it, Lloyd?" she asked as they entered and closed the door. They still didn't dare let the dog out on her own; it wasn't that she would flee human company, because she loved it. It was that she might follow her nose too avidly and get into trouble.

"It's the attic! There *is* one. Obsidian sniffed the stair, only there wasn't anything there, until I found the switch in the wall. I'll show you." He was as eager as the dog.

"You must show me," Chandelle said, knowing that the boy would not be able to rest until he had.

They went upstairs, into the hall. There Lloyd stroked his hand along the wall, and suddenly there was color forming and intensifying, until a staircase was there. "But it's not real, at first," Lloyd said. "Touch it, Grandma!"

She humored him, putting her hand on the stair's railing. And her hand passed right through it. "Oh!"

"It's a holo! But I can make it real. Watch." He touched the wall again, and the stairway became illuminated. "Try it now."

She touched the stair—and it was solid. "This is certainly interesting, Lloyd," she said. That was the understatement of the morning. "And you say there is an attic up there?"

"Yeah. Full of—I don't know whats. But I guess we'll be figuring it all out."

"Surely so. This house is full of surprises." That was perhaps the understatement of the month.

Llynn appeared. "What's going on? Oh—you found a stairway up!"

Lloyd started explaining it all to her. Chandelle excused herself and went down to the kitchen. The attic did indeed look interesting, but she had work to do.

After that the attic was everything. Lloyd, Llynn, and Penn seemed equally fascinated by it. They rushed through breakfast and mounted the stair, and their exclamations issued fairly steadily from the upper reaches. This, despite the fact that none of them had any idea what any of the artifacts were, or what they might do. Periodically one of them would come down to make a report.

"We've found instructions, we think," Llynn announced. "But they're in alien script, or something. It looks like little squiggles. I copied some of them out so I can study them in better light." She showed the sheet, spreading it out on the kitchen table.

Chandelle looked at it. They were indeed squiggly lines and loops. "Could it be glyphic?" she asked.

"Glyphic?"

"Formed of glyphs. Symbols that represent the objects they relate to. Tiny simplified, stylized pictures. Like the ancient Egyptian writing."

The girl considered. "Maybe so. They do look like little pictures, in a way, if I let my imagination work." She ran her finger across the paper, picking out particular figures. "Here's one maybe like a sailboat, and another like a sleeping dog, and—" She paused.

"There's a problem?"

"Uh, not exactly. It just—but maybe not."

Chandelle looked. The squiggle was tiny, but was oddly suggestive of a naked man in a state of sexual excitement. "Maybe not," she agreed.

Llynn got up from the table. "I'll go copy some more. Maybe some of them will make more sense." She left the kitchen.

Chandelle contemplated the sheet of paper on the table. The more she looked at it, the more suggestive the squiggle figures became. It was almost as if they were telling a story. As if a man and a dog were sailing on a sailboat, and the man saw a woman—twin circles were highly suggestive of bare breasts—and suffered a masculine reaction. So he brought his craft to shore, but by then the woman was gone.

Chandelle looked away, then returned to the paper. Now the squiggles were meaningless. Yet for a moment there had seemed to be a story there. Was it just her foolish imagination, or was this the message of the squiggles? How could she tell?

She rotated the paper, viewing the squiggles sideways. Of course she didn't know which way was up, for them, or whether there *was* a proper orientation. These were just copies Llynn had drawn, perhaps not accurate. Yet there was something about the little figures.

Her vision clouded, and the figures blurred, then seemed to assume new configurations. Now there seemed to be not a sailboat, but a—a spaceship, traveling toward twin circular planets and aiming a space cannon at them. But by the time it got within range, the planets had disappeared.

She blinked, and the paper contained only meaningless squiggles again. But she wondered. She was not unduly given to flights of fantasy. Why did these tiny figures have such power to incite her notions? Was she simply tired, or was there something to it?

She turned the paper again, so that now it was upside down, or at least inverted. She fixed her gaze on it, and let her vision blur. Now there seemed to be a building with odd architecture, or perhaps a pavilion that was mostly a roof supported by a central pylon. Under that roof was a hanging effigy. The neighboring picture expanded that figure, which seemed to be diving into chaos. Nearby was a plant with two round flowers. Perhaps the flowers would bring that effigy to life, but they wilted before the swimmer arrived.

Chandelle looked up. She glanced at her watch, and was

startled to see that half an hour had passed. She had been lost in her fancies about the squiggle sketches. This was not like her. It was time to take a break.

At that point Penn came down. "I'm convinced that these are operative devices," he said. "But we can't figure out what they are supposed to do."

"Llynn brought down a paper with representations of glyphs she said you found up there."

"Yes, she is copying more of them. Each device has its own instructions, assuming that's what they are. But we can't make head or tail of them."

"But they are suggestive."

"Are they?" He glanced at the paper on the table. "They look like random scribblings to me."

"Have you tried concentrating on them for a while?"

"No, I've been concentrating on the devices themselves, trying to get some hint. And failing. But I'm sure they are functional in some fashion. After all, everything in this house has proved to be functional, often in amazing ways, once we understand them."

"Could there be a—a written language that requires imaginative interpretation?"

"I suppose so," he agreed. "I must get back up there."

He would have to take time with the squiggles to understand her point. And she couldn't be sure she was right. So there was no point in pushing that aspect. "I think I'll take Obsidian out for a walk. Suppose we explore a new setting?"

Penn shrugged and walked with her to the back door. "What one would you like?"

"Maybe the future."

"There are several futures. I doubt that any of them are real, because that could lead to paradox. We couldn't bring anything back from the future, because that might enable us to change that future. They are probably just models, to show us what may be coming, years, or decades, or centuries from now."

"Yes. Maybe the alien village. That intrigues me, as long as I don't see an actual alien."

He set the panel at 1. "I won't change it until you're safely back inside. Are you sure you want to go alone?"

"Alone? Hardly! I'll have Obsidian."

"Oh. Of course. But don't be too long. I'm sure it's safe, but—"

"I know. There remain so many mysteries to fathom. So it's best to tread cautiously."

"Exactly." He kissed her.

Then she called the dog, and snapped the leash to her collar. "We have a surprise for you this time, Obsidian," she said. The dog wagged her tail.

Chandelle opened the door, and they lurched out, for the dog know only one way to take a walk: straining ever forward. She wasn't well trained, but her perpetual enthusiasm made up for it.

The alien village was empty, of course; otherwise Chandelle would never have ventured into it. They assumed it was a village; actually it was a series of linked structures that were more suggestive of supports for a flower arrangement than of housing. So maybe this was a garden. How could they know?

Obsidian hurried along what seemed to be a path that wound between the structures, avidly sniffing. Chandelle noticed that the ground beside the path was not solid; it was perforated by many deep holes. She tried to see to the bottom of some, but they curved into darkness. Each was no more than four inches across. Drainage? Yet there seemed to be no channels for water. In fact, the ground was uneven, and the holes were in the slopes rather than in the bottoms. Did this make any sense?

Then she saw something else. There was a curving wall—and on that wall was a series of squiggles.

She stopped and stared. The glyphs in the attic—also here? Did that mean there was a more significant connection between this setting and the house than just a scene for them to look at? That the creatures who lived here might be the ones who made the house? If so—

Her mind balked at the implications. So she concentrated on the glyphs. They were definitely the same sort as the ones Llynn had copied. But every squiggle was different. Like snowflakes, no two were quite the same. There was actually considerable variety in their shapes.

Obsidian pulled at the leash, but Chandelle was fascinated by the figures on the wall, and couldn't leave them yet. Was this a monument of some kind, commemorating some great alien accomplishment? Or was it a message for visitors like herself?

The figures were sharper than the ones Llynn had drawn; they had more character. They started to come alive as she stared at them. None resembled men or women, or ships, or anything else associated with human beings. But her limited experience with Llynn's sheet had prepared her to see what they showed.

The wall fuzzed, and she was looking at a three dimensional representation of—the alien village. She knew it was made of squiggles on the plane of the wall, but now it looked real. More than real; it was as if she stood in the original village, rather than the mere setting that this one was.

It became an animation. She saw a level stretch of ground, featureless. She wasn't sure whether it was earth or stone. Then a spot appeared in it, expanding into a circle. From the circle rose a lump or the nose of a cone. No, it was the snout of a living creature. In fact it was a worm. A weird metallic worm, but nevertheless a worm; it lengthened and thinned in the manner of a worm. A large glossy worm.

The worm paused, casting about as if surveying the terrain to be sure there were no birds nearby. Then its head contracted and extruded gray goo. This formed a bubble over the hole as the worm's head retreated into the ground.

After a moment the bubble heaved, and the tip of the snout of the worm rose up through its center. The gray substance widened into a ring fastened to the ground, congealing in place. Now it was like a tiny volcano, with the worm inside.

The worm paused again in reflection, then performed another contraction and extrusion. Another bubble formed, and was in due course converted to a ring as the worm poked through its center and shaped it above the first ring. It was forming a gray tower.

Another point appeared in the ground, becoming another circle. A second worm was rising. It went through a similar series of operations, except that its rising tower was yellow.

Then there were many worms working in the area, shaping their structures. The action accelerated, not because they were working faster but because the presentation was being foreshortened for economy of assimilation. Their multi-colored towers rose up in graceful stems, curves, and spirals, and merged to form arches and suspended knots. It became a network of intertwining columns, and finally a section of an alien village like the one she was visiting now.

The worms were architects, living *inside* the columns and connections. That was why the village had seemed so hard to fathom; what she had taken for weird living space was actually the interstices, not used.

Chandelle came out of her vision and looked around. And gasped.

Obsidian was gone. The dog had somehow slipped her collar during Chandelle's inattention, and headed out on her own exploration while Chandelle was distracted by the glyphs on the wall. Who knew where the animal was now?

"Obsidian!" she called, but there was no response. In a developing panic, she cast about, searching for any sign of the dog. There was none.

Chandelle realized that she needed help. She would be unlikely to find Obsidian on her own; there was too much of the labyrinthine village. The others could spread out and cover much more territory.

She hurried back to the house. Lynne was in the kitchen with more sheets of paper. "I lost Obsidian!" Chandelle cried. "She slipped her collar while I was distracted."

"Uh-oh. I'll fetch the others." Llynn got up and ran out of the room.

In moments Penn and Lloyd were there. "What happened?" Penn asked.

Chandelle blurted it out, barely organized. In the process she forgot to tell what she had seen in the squiggle wall. That hardly seemed relevant, as long as the dog was missing.

"I think the three of us can handle it," Penn said. "You should remain in the house, Chandelle, just in case." That was their standard policy: to keep someone in the house at all times. Because it did disappear from all the back yard settings, and could be hard to locate. Not all of them had boulders to mark its place.

They went out, and Chandelle remained in the house. She was appalled that she had been so careless to let the dog get away. Of course Obsidian had followed her nose; that's why the leash was necessary. Yet the squiggles had been so intriguing. The setting might be dead, but that alien writing was alive.

Her eye fell on the sheets of paper Llynn had left. She sat at the table and focused on them. Even though the sketched copies were imperfect, they carried the magic of the form. In a moment she was "reading" them.

The top page showed a man putting on what appeared to be a headband. Then he looked out across a vast landscape where many odd things appeared.

Chandelle considered. This was a copy of a series of glyphs that appeared in one section of the attic. Could it be the instructions for one of the artifacts there? A band that the worms had made to enable them to see?

She looked at the next sheet. After a moment those squiggles came to life. This time a woman was putting on a pair of boots. Then she took a step—and was suddenly across the page, leaving a chain of dust balls behind.

That could be seven league boots. Put them on, and travel fast and far without a car. She wasn't sure how a worm could use them, but these were obviously made for people. Maybe the worms were in business, making things for other species. Maybe they traded, getting supplies in return, or perhaps services they needed.

She tried the third sheet. This showed a man putting on a radio headset, or maybe just a pair of ear muffs. Then he cocked his head, evidently listening. A bubble appeared above his head, and in it there formed an object—no, another person, a woman. She was speaking, because there were sound waves at her mouth. And across the page was that woman, in a larger representation, speaking with identical waves. That must be the woman the man was hearing. Then the thought bubble above the man changed to what looked like a machine, also making sound. Across the page was a similar machine with similar sound. So the man could hear that too, when he wanted to. A third squiggle showed him thinking of a running river, and there was a river elsewhere, too.

Chandelle's pulse got stronger. If this meant what she thought it did, there was a set of earphones in the attic that would enable her to hear anything she wanted to hear, no matter how distant. Including a lost dog.

She got up and went to the stairs. There was the plaque, and the number was 7. It had been 6 this morning, after Lloyd found the attic. That suggested that her revelation was a true discovery. She had learned to read the alien script, and the house knew.

She went upstairs, and the attic stairs were gone. She suffered an instant of panic, then realized that Penn could have turned it off as he departed. Or maybe it turned itself off when no one was in the attic and it wasn't being used for more than a few minutes. This house was thoughtful in many little ways, and that could be one of them.

She stroked her fingers along the wall until she found the hidden indentation, and pushed its button. The stairs appeared. She pushed it again, and they solidified. This was marvelous technology, and she liked it, as she got used to it. She wouldn't mind living in this house permanently, despite aspects that made her nervous. As with a car, it became less dangerous as a person learned better how to use it.

She climbed into the lighted attic. She had forgotten to take the sheets of squiggles with her, but it didn't matter; she would read the originals. She peered at the objects that lined the walls. And saw one that resembled a set of ear muffs.

She went to it. Sure enough, the glyphs were those Llynn had copied, only these were more artistically drawn. Their effect was stronger. Now that she knew how, she could readily read them.

She picked up the headset, and paused. Were there any cautions? And dangers, or at least things to be careful about? So she looked again at the glyphs.

Yes, the man, after thinking of several things, tried to think of two at once. Then he fell down, with a throbbing head. So it was best to focus on just one thing at a time. And to keep one's eyes open; when the man closed his, he walked into a tree. Understood.

She carried the set down to the kitchen. There she nerved herself and put it carefully on.

Nothing happened. After a moment she realized why: she wasn't thinking of anything she wanted to hear. So she thought of Penn. Still nothing. Did that mean it wasn't working, or that he wasn't talking at the moment?

She banished Penn and tried Lloyd.

"Hey, you dumb mutt! Where are you?"

She jumped, thinking he had come into the kitchen behind her. But no one was there. It was the headset, tuning in on his words as he searched for Obsidian.

Very well, then. She let Lloyd go and tuned in on the dog. And heard a faint whimpering.

She got up and went to the door—and hesitated. She shouldn't leave the house empty; that was their agreement. Yet the dog was suffering, or at least unhappy; should she make her wait for rescue?

She decided that this was a suitable exception to their rule. She would go out to find Obsidian, then locate the others, and explain.

She left the house, keeping the dog in mind. The whimpering was so clear as to seem close, but she knew it wasn't. She oriented on it and walked carefully along a path through the alien village, eyes wide open. She wasn't sure whether she could hear other things while orienting on the distant sounds, so it was better to watch everything around her.

She picked the best route she could find through the alien architecture. She appreciated the colored structures much better, now that she understood how they were made and used. She would want to learn more about the worms, in due course. But right now she had to rescue Obsidian.

Soon the sounds became not louder, but somehow clearer, as if she were getting better definition as she got closer. Their position seemed to shift, and she realized that this was because as she got closer, any deviation from the direct way toward them made a larger difference.

She came to a large wormhole, one big enough for a man to crawl into. She had thought of the worms as small, but of course that wasn't necessarily the case. Some of the vermicular structures were huge.

From the dark depth of this hole, the sounds of the dog came. "Obsidian!" she called, and was rewarded by a frantic barking. She had found the dog—to a degree. But what was she to do about it now? She did not want to climb down that hole and perhaps get trapped herself.

It was time to get help. "We're coming, Obsidian!" she called down the hole. Then she tuned the earmuffs to Penn. He was still silent, as he tended to be. She tried Llynn, and heard her, but she seemed far away. The alien headset did somehow give an indication of distance, though she wasn't sure how. She just knew. So she tried Lloyd again.

"Where are you, mutt?" The call sounded more desperate; the boy was really getting worried. But the important thing was that he was close.

"Lloyd!" she called as loudly as she could.

He heard her. "Grandma! What you doing out here?"

"Finding your dog. Come here."

In a moment he came running into view. "Hey, you got one of the things in the attic!"

"It's a hearing aid. It enabled me to orient on the dog from a distance. Obsidian's down that wormhole." She pointed.

"Hey, girl, you there?" he called.

There was a renewed flurry of barking. She recognized his voice, all right.

"I better go down," Lloyd said. "Only—"

"Only how will you get back up, if she can't?" Chandelle finished for him. "We'll need to study this more carefully."

"Yeah. Maybe Grandpa can figure out a way."

"Yes. Do you know where he is? And Llynn?"

"No. We got separated. But maybe I can find them, if—" He looked at the headset, quick to recognize its advantage.

"Very well." She removed the muffs and handed them to him. "You think of the person you want to hear. But only one person at a time, or you may get a headache. And watch where's you're going."

"Got it, Grandma." He donned the set, paused, then took off running.

Meanwhile Chandelle studied the local layout. There were several other large holes, and some slanted downward less abruptly. Maybe there was one a person could safely navigate. But probably they would need a safety line. It might be easy to get lost down there, if the wormholes intersected each other; it could be like a huge maze.

Lloyd returned, with Penn puffing after him. "You used an alien artifact to find Obsidian?" he asked. "That's amazing." He was holding the ear muffs.

"I deciphered their script," she said. "Their glyphs. They told me how to use the hearing aid."

"And so not only have we found Obsidian, we have gained a valuable new tool," he said, kissing her. "But now we have to get the dog out of the hole."

"I'll get a rope from the house," Lloyd said, and dashed off again.

"Meanwhile, we'd better locate Llynn," Chandelle said, pleased by his recognition of her success.

"Let's see how these work on me," he said, and put them on. "Llynn, where are you?" After a pause, he glanced at Chandelle. "I don't hear her."

"Keep listening," she said. "Maybe she'll speak." Then she cupped her hands to her mouth and called: "Llynn!"

"She heard you," Penn said. "She's answering."

Chandelle didn't hear anything, but was satisfied. "Over here!" she called.

"She's coming." And soon she did hear the approach of the girl.

"What's going on?" Llynn asked. "Did you find her?"

"Yes," Chandelle said. "Down there." She pointed at the hole.

"Ooo! No wonder we couldn't find her.'

While they waited for Lloyd, they surveyed the pattern of wormholes, and Chandelle caught Llynn up on what she had discovered. "So it was your drawings that did it," she concluded, careful to give the girl credit.

"And I never caught on," Llynn said ruefully. "I was trying to find a pattern, like letters of the alphabet. I didn't realize that the key was in how they looked. I thought that one man was just my dirty mind."

"Your mind was clean. The image was dirty." Chandelle considered a moment. "Of course it isn't really dirty, just—"

"I know, Grandma. Just awkward."

Lloyd returned with a coil of rope. "So how do we do this?" he asked. "Maybe tie it to my foot, so you can drag me back?"

"That seems awkward and uncomfortable," Chandelle said. She was not at all easy with the idea of him descending into that hole, but neither did she want to leave Obsidian down there.

"We'll anchor you mountain climbing style," Penn said. "With a loop around your waist, slack. If you fall, it will support you. If you don't, it won't get in your way. Meanwhile, I will listen to you on the hearing aid, so you won't need to yell. Just speak normally and I will hear you. I will have to shout to reach you, however."

"Let me use the hearing aid," Chandelle said. "That will give you greater freedom of action."

Penn shrugged. "Very well." He removed the earpiece and gave it to her.

"Okay." The boy stood while Penn made a carefully knotted loop of rope resembling a belt. Then he climbed into the hole, feet first. Chandelle marveled that he didn't seem concerned. But he was young; perhaps claustrophobia came with age and relative infirmity.

"I hear you," Penn said down the hole, not needing the hearing aid initially. "Can you hear me? Good. Now don't rush it; feel your way carefully until you reach her."

They remained in touch, while Chandelle and Llynn watched. "And you say worms made all this?" Llynn asked.

"Yes. I saw in on the wall. I think it must be an instruction sheet for us to find, so we would know the background of this setting."

"But worms couldn't have built the house."

"I think they coordinate with other species. After all, they don't live on Earth."

"In earth, not on Earth," Llynn agreed. "But we still don't know what they want with us." She glanced at the hole. "Is he okay down there?"

Chandelle remembered to orient on the boy. Immediately the sounds came, so close and real that it was almost as though she were down there herself. She closed her eyes, attuning further. "I'll see," she said.

Indeed, it was as if she were seeing, for there was darkness all around and the sounds became all that identified the participants. Lloyd was breathing hard, with little grunts as he squirmed on down, and he was muttering to himself. "No freak, no freak. Gotta get Obsidian. No freak."

He *was* frightened! He had concealed it from them, but now that he was alone he was having a tough time not freaking out. But he was carrying on with the mission. Bratty he might be, but here in the crunch he was showing courage.

Chandelle thought to orient on the dog. Suddenly it was as if Obsidian were right next to her, fidgeting, breathing rapidly, making faint splashes. "Obsidian is in water," she announced, opening her eyes.

Penn glanced at her. "I think Lloyd's near there by now," he said. "It must be slippery below, so she couldn't scramble out. Is she all right?"

"Yes, I think so. She's uncomfortable, maybe cold, but not in actual physical pain."

"It must be awful, caught in the dark," Llynn said, looking a bit drawn.

Chandelle closed her eyes again. She was still with the dog, and her identification seemed to be intensifying. Hearing was translating to feeling. Maybe she heard shivering, because she felt cold. And—

And something else. A sound not of the dog. Was it merely the lapping of the water?

"Get her out of there!" she cried, a tinge of panic in her voice. "There's something *with* her."

"Lloyd!" Penn shouted down the hole. "Get your business done quickly."

Now the boy was close; Obsidian was making squeaks of eager greeting. They touched, and there was the sound of a hand being slurped. "He's there," Chandelle said. "Touching the dog's head."

"Take off the loop of rope," Penn called. "Brace your legs against the sides of the passage. Put the loop over her body, behind the front legs. Tighten it just enough to hold. Then hang on to the rope yourself, in front of her, and we'll haul you both up. Don't get behind the dog; don't go into the water."

Acting on Penn's instructions, Lloyd tied the rope around the dog. Chandelle seemed to feel the rope about her own midriff. "It's snug," she said.

Then Penn slowly hauled on the rope. Obsidian scrambled, helping herself, with Lloyd urging her on. With the support of the rope, they could handle the slippery slope.

But something was following. "Faster!" Chandelle cried.

"We don't want to hurt them," Penn said.

"Then pull faster! They aren't alone."

Llynn joined Penn, and the two of them pulled more vigorously on the rope. There was a whine of pain, but the dog was as eager as anyone to get clear of the depths. Now any sounds of possible pursuit were lost in the clamor of scrambling feet and hard breathing.

Then they climbed to the ground level, and finally made it out of the hole. Llynn dropped the rope and hugged the boy, who for once didn't object. "That was close!" Lloyd gasped. "There was something down there."

"We know," Penn said. "That's why we had to hurry."

"What was it?" Llynn asked.

"Mostly a feeling," Lloyd admitted. "But it was getting awful strong."

Chandelle hugged Obsidian, and rubbed her wet legs, while Penn untied the rope. There was no sign of whatever had been behind them. Could it have been imagination? There had not been anything moving in any of the backdoor settings, before. Yet how could they have taken the chance of waiting too long?

"I heard something with the hearing aid," Chandelle said. "I don't know what it was. Maybe just the water moving of itself. Maybe I'm just a hysterical woman."

"Maybe," Penn said. But he did not look satisfied with that.

They were all back together again. But after this, Chandelle would make very sure not to let the dog get loose.

Chapter 6
Moscow

Penn considered the pages of squiggle glyphs Llynn had copied. Chandelle had figured out the key, and the plaque had advanced another number, but there remained a lot to learn. Even with the instructions, some of those alien artifacts were impenetrable. For example there was what looked like a variation of the hearing aid, a circlet of wire that hooked over one ear. They had all tried it, but it made no difference to ordinary hearing, and did not tune in on distant sounds. So either it didn't work, or they were not reading the instructions correctly. The squiggles seemed to suggest that it did facilitate the hearing of the person who wore it, at least in that ear. But it did not. The other artifacts they had considered were similarly confusing.

Now Penn was diverting himself by mapping the settings of the front door. There were hundreds, but all seemed to be cities. If this were straight geographical travel, what were the chances that it would always land on a city? Very small, he was sure. So they had all been zeroed in, probably so that the house could sit on an existing address in each city, and be inconspicuous. A lot of work mist have gone into that! Were there hundreds of houses, or were the lots empty when the house was elsewhere?

"Bet I know what you're thinking, Grandpa," Llynn said behind him. "You figure the cities are real, but how about the house?"

"Yes. It doesn't seem to move when we change settings. But if it doesn't, that suggests that this is a—a tesseract."

"A what?"

"A tesseract. A four dimensional cube. It's a mathematical concept, impossible to make in reality. But in this instance, it could mean that this same house is everywhere, and that when we change the setting, we are merely focusing on another of its existing faces."

"So how do we tell?"

"I can think of a way, perhaps, but it might be risky."

"Like stepping outside when the house goes away?" she asked.

"Yes. Of course it would return immediately. Still—"

"We could test it by putting something out there, leaving it, and returning. If it's still there—"

"Now there's a notion," he agreed. "We could put out a clock, and see if it kept the same time."

"Coming up," she said, removing her wristwatch.

"Oh, I didn't mean to risk your property."

"I know, Grandpa. But I don't think it's much of a risk. Pick a city."

"Here's Moscow. It's night; there's not much action there at the moment. So it should be relatively safe to experiment." He set the panel at 100, and the city appeared.

She opened the door and stepped quickly out. She set the watch on the front step, then reconsidered and took it farther out, to get beyond the ambiance of the house.

When she was safely back inside, he reset the door to Philadelphia. Then to Okinawa. Then back to Moscow. She went out and got her watch. "It's still keeping time," she said, putting it on her wrist. She paused outside the door. "But I'm not sure that's enough."

He had a notion what she meant. It made him nervous. "Get back in here and we'll discuss it."

"No, I'll stay out here this time. You take the house on the same tour, and then I'll report what I saw."

"But Llynn, if we're wrong—"

"Then I'm in trouble. But I don't think we are. Do it, Grandpa; I'm not coming in."

His hands were sweating. "Llynn, please—"

"You always knew I was a willful girl. This is something we've got to find out. Go."

He stared at her, standing defiantly in her shirt and jeans. Should he go out there and try to haul her in? She might run down the street, and he wouldn't be able to catch her. It was better to avoid that scene. Yet if he did it, and she wasn't there when he returned, what then?

"Go," she repeated, stepping away from the house.

He closed the door and reset the panel, quickly, before the enormity of the risk overcame him. Philadelphia appeared. Then Okinawa. Then Moscow again.

She was there. Relief made him weak. He opened the door. "Get in here, Llynn!"

This time she came in. "You did the tour?"

"Yes! What did you see?"

"Nothing, Grandpa. The house is locally styled, and it didn't change."

"I suppose that's the way it has to be. If a house suddenly appeared and disappeared, it would quickly attract attention. But this doesn't answer our question."

"Yes. We need more. Why don't you go again, and I'll try to enter the house while you're gone?"

"I can't do that! The risk—suppose you were there when the house returned?"

She nodded. "Could be bad. So we'd better bring in the others." She left the room.

"Wait, Llynn!" he protested, too late.

In a moment Chandelle and Lloyd were there. "You left her outside?" Chandelle demanded, appalled.

"Oh, come on Grandma," the girl said. "This is stuff we have to know."

"Not at the risk of your life!" Chandelle said severely.

"It's not as if it was anything important," Lloyd said, smirking.

"Shut up, or I'll make you dance again," Llynn said, nudging him.

"Stop pushing me around." But it was evident that the edge had gone from their rivalry; they were only teasing.

"I know I shouldn't have done it," Penn said.

"Look, Grandma, we don't want to get caught again by what we don't know about," Llynn said persuasively. "We rescued Obsidian, but next time it could be worse. We need to figure things out early, before there's trouble, so we know what to expect."

"Not by leaving you outside while the house travels."

"But how else can we find out? Something happens to this house, and we'd better understand it. It may even be part of the testing we get graded on by the stair plaque."

That made Chandelle pause. Lloyd stepped in. "Next time it's my turn. Llynn can't have all the fun."

Chandelle looked warily at them. "Are you united in this?"

"I suspect we are," Penn said. "It could be a greater risk to occupy this house without exploring the ramifications of its potentials."

"Then don't do it alone," she said. "Do it in pairs—and one stay clear while the other explores."

That seemed reasonable. "Agreed," Penn said. He glanced at the others. Llynn and Lloyd both nodded.

They set it up with Penn and Llynn taking the next turn, a brief walk—through. They stepped out the front door, and stood on the walk while Lloyd moved the house. Penn felt a nervous thrill; this really was exciting.

"Want me to hold your hand, Grandpa?" Llynn inquired mischievously. "I'm more experienced in this."

"Yes," he said, smiling.

She took his hand, and it really did make him feel better. Two could face the unknown with more courage than one.

Nothing changed. "Didn't they do it?"

"They're doing it," she said. "It just doesn't show. Which I guess is the way it has to be, so as not to attract attention."

The light in the house went out. “Except for that?” he asked.

“Except for that,” she agreed. “Can’t have a light on in a house that isn’t there.”

“That’s all there is to it? No implosion of air, no—”

“No nothing,” she said firmly.

After a moment the light came on again. Then the door opened. “Are you all right?” Chandelle called.

“Nothing to it,” Penn called back.

“My turn!” Lloyd cried, dashing out.

Llynn walked back to the house. At the door she turned. “How long do we give you?”

Penn glanced at his watch. “Five minutes should do it,” he said.

“Five minutes,” she agreed, glancing at her own watch. Then she entered and closed the door behind her.

“Wait until the light goes out,” Penn cautioned the boy. “And we must be sure to vacate before the time is up.”

“Gotcha. We don’t want them landing on our heads.” Lloyd seemed to have no added concern for the possible risk of the maneuver. Probably it was considerably less scary for him than crawling into a dark wormhole had been.

The light disappeared. They stepped forward. Penn felt the thrill of nervous excitement again. This was—this was perhaps testing fate.

Lloyd yanked open the screen door. He tried to open the main door, but it would not budge. “Hey—it’s locked!”

Penn hadn’t thought of that. He produced his key card. But there was no place for it. The door had a conventional old fashioned key hole, and he had no mechanical key. “Locked when the occupants are away,” he said. “That does make sense.”

“Let’s try the back door,” Lloyd said, heading around the house.

Penn followed, as he did not want to let the boy get out of sight in the darkness.

It was the same story with the back door. So they tried a window. It would not budge. They were completely locked out.

They returned to the front and waited until the light returned. "Are you all right?" Chandelle asked, clearly worried.

"We couldn't get in," Lloyd said. "Doors are locked."

They discussed it, and concluded that the house might occupy a frame set in Moscow, or any other city, and be completely closed off except when the house "occupied" it. So that there could be no intruders. If someone broke in, that would probably trigger an alarm that would prevent the house from phasing in, until it was fixed. They agreed that they did not want to try to break in.

"So I suppose we have an answer, of sorts," Penn said. "There are houses in many cities, but they are mere blocks reserving the space for the real one. They—"

"Something's happening out there," Lloyd said, peering out.

Penn looked. Someone was running in the night. "Perhaps we should vacate."

"No, wait," Llynn said. "It's a man, and somebody's chasing him."

Indeed, three men were in pursuit of a lone figure. Even in the darkness, they looked like rough brutes, while the fugitive seemed pitiful. He had a fair lead, but was faltering, evidently worn out.

"Street gang," Lloyd said. "Found a mark."

"We've got to help him," Llynn exclaimed, pushing out the door.

"No!" Chandelle cried. But Llynn was already on her way.

Penn went after her, knowing he couldn't stop her from doing what she had in mind. To get involved in a street-crime in progress—this could be disaster.

"Here!" Llynn cried to the man.

He saw her, and swerved toward her. She ran back toward the house, beckoning. She was bringing the man inside!

She ran by Penn, and the man followed, staggering. Penn saw a dark patch on his clothing. That looked like blood. He intercepted the man, put one arm around him, and urged him through the door. Lloyd slammed the door behind them.

Penn eased the fugitive to the floor. "He's wounded," he said as the man lay down, barely conscious. "Knifed, I think."

"Oh!" Llynn gasped, seeing the blood.

"I'll get a bandage," Chandelle said, hurrying off.

Penn looked up. "Lloyd, change the setting."

"Gotcha." The boy reached for the panel.

But the pursuit was too close. The lead man struck the door, crashing it open. He tumbled into the house, and the other two followed.

Then for a moment the tableau froze. One intruder was sitting on the floor, the two others standing behind him, staring at Llynn and the fugitive. Lloyd stood by the door, not daring to touch the panel now. And Penn stared stupidly back at the men. How was he going to handle this disaster? The three were young and brutish, and they did have knives. How could they be gotten out?

What about the undo button on the wall? Could that reverse the intrusion? But he realized immediately that it couldn't, because it would affect only the actions of the house, not the people.

Then the man sitting on the floor spoke. It was Russian, but too fast for Penn to fathom. The other two did, though. One turned and grabbed Lloyd, while the other drew his knife and strode forward to menace Penn with it. Penn just stood there, knowing that any motion could get him killed. He could not match the speed and power of the young thug, and even had that been possible, what of Lloyd and Llynn?

The seated man sprang to his feet and advanced on Llynn. She screamed and backed away. Satisfied for the moment, the man turned to Penn and rapped out some kind of query.

"I'm sorry, I don't understand," Penn said. He was trying to judge what he might accomplish if he took them by surprise. He could kick the nearest man in the groin and get his knife, but that was not enough.

The man spoke to the one holding Lloyd. He pushed the boy into Llynn and went out of the room.

"What do you want with us?" Penn said, not having to feign fear.

The leader grunted something, evidently not understanding. So Penn took a risk. "Timorous girl, terrified boy," he said in the same tone of query he had used before. "Helpless old man. They don't know about Chandelle—or Obsidian."

"Nyet!" the man rapped. So Penn shut up. But he had already gotten his message out. They had roles to play, until they could find a way to get out of this fix.

The wounded man lay where he had fallen, unconscious. No help there.

The missing man returned from the garage with cord. He used lengths of it to tie Penn and Lloyd. This was bad; the two of them didn't dare resist, yet they would be helpless when bound.

They had no choice. They submitted as the man competently tied their hands and feet. They were perforce out of the action.

There was a sound at the back of the house. Immediately the leader was alert. He realized that there was another person in the house. He snapped an order, and the other two charged out to locate Chandelle. Obviously they intended to rob the house, having discovered it in the course of their pursuit of the fugitive. But they could not afford to have someone loose in the house, to summon help. They didn't know that the family knew no one in Moscow to whom they could appeal. Or that the house itself could disappear from Moscow, trapping the intruders in another part of the world. If the inhabitants ever got a chance to move it.

The back door slammed. Chandelle had gone out the back! Maybe she thought to hide until the intruders left. But Penn wasn't sure. Certainly she wasn't safe in the house. But suppose the setting got changed, stranding her in the ancient forest? Penn was not at all easy with this.

The back door slammed again, surely because one of the men

was going after her.

Meanwhile the leader had a notion about Llynn. He sheathed his knife and grabbed her by the arm. She screamed and pulled ineffectively away, being the timorous girl. Because as long as there was another thug in the house, it wasn't safe to attack the leader.

The man hauled her in and grabbed her other arm. He tried to kiss her. She screamed again and turned her face away. Penn strained at his bonds, but could not get free. Lloyd looked just as uncomfortable. But what they do?

Llynn would have to help herself. "If you have to, knee him in the groin," he told her, risking the wrath of her captor. "Then flee to the attic."

The man was tearing at her jeans, in his eagerness not making much progress. Llynn faced Penn momentarily and nodded; she was struggling, but she was aware. When she got her opportunity, she would strike.

There was a shout from the rear of the house. Penn could guess its nature: there was something funny about the back door.

The leader shouted something back, and paused, listening. After a moment the back door slammed a third time: the second man going out after the first, to fetch him back.

The leader returned his attention to Llynn. This time he grabbed a handful of her shirt and yanked it open. She screamed again, the very picture of a fainting female. But Penn knew she couldn't stall much longer. Soon the man's attack would go too far—and how could they stop it without putting all of them at worse risk?

But it was the man who stalled. He was becoming aware that the other two men had not returned, and he didn't like that. So he decided to check on them before finishing with the girl. He headed for the back of the house, dragging Llynn along.

Then Chandelle tiptoed in the other door, with Obsidian on a short leash. "Those other two are gone," she said. "I'll untie you."

She fumbled with Penn's bonds. But they were well knotted, and she wasn't making much progress.

"Don't fool with it," he said urgently, "Just cut the cord."

"Oh, of course! I didn't think. I didn't bring a knife."

Meanwhile Obsidian was licking Lloyd's face. She didn't understand about him being tied.

Then the leader returned, still dragging Llynn. They heard him coming though the adjacent room.

"Sid! Hide!" Lloyd said. The dog ran behind the television set and hunched down, hiding, thinking it was a game.

Chandelle, still trying to untie Penn, didn't hear the thug until too late. She turned just as the man entered, dragging a disheveled Llynn. "Oh!"

The man made an exclamation. "Get down," Penn said. "Be helpless." He wished she had thought to bring a knife, but of course she had been distracted by the threat to them all. Even so, her ploy had almost worked.

The man snapped words at Penn, gesturing toward the back of the house.

Oh. It was dark in Moscow, but light in the ancient forest. And with the other two out there—but why hadn't they come back in?

"I changed the setting," Chandelle murmured.

Brilliant! That had isolated the men, so than now there was only the one to deal with. But how were they to do that? Chandelle and Llynn were the only ones not tied, and they would not be able to fight the brute.

Still, the odds were better than they had been. Maybe they could trick him into going out the back door too. Except for the problem of language.

The man spoke again, surely demanding to know what had happened to his two minions. When Penn couldn't answer, the thug drew his knife and menaced Llynn with it.

This was getting serious. "They're gone," Penn said quickly.

"And you'd better go too. You don't know what you're getting into, with this house." But of course the man didn't understand.

The man raised his knife toward Llynn's head. She flinched. She must have forgotten his prior advice. Penn faced the man, as if addressing him, but spoke to Llynn: "If he tries to cut you, kick him in the groin and get clear of him. Run out the back door if you have to."

"I've got a better way," Lloyd said. "Watch."

"Don't antagonize him!" Penn said, alarmed. "You're helpless."

"No I'm not. Not any more." The boy faced the man. "Hey, poop-breath! Look at me!"

The tone conveyed the message. The man looked at Lloyd.

"Okay, crap-head," the boy continued. "Try this on for size." He made a face and stuck out his tongue. That transcended language.

"Lloyd!" Chandelle cried, appalled at the mischief he was inciting. Penn echoed the sentiment. Had the boy gone crazy?

The man realized that he was being insulted. "Nyet!" he said.

In response, Lloyd gave him the Bronx cheer.

The man strode toward him, lifting his free hand, dragging Llynn behind.

Lloyd screamed as if struck.

Obsidian came out of her hiding place like a vengeful genie. Growling, she leaped at the man, catching his arm in her teeth. She was ninety six and a half pounds of fury.

Suddenly Penn understood the boy's strategy. If there was one time when the dog wouldn't be friendly, it was when her master was attacked. Lloyd had incited that attack.

But the man was no fainting flower. He let go of Llynn and whirled on the dog, reaching for his knife.

Now Llynn was free to fight. She kicked at his groin. But her foot bounced off the man's thigh.

"Go get a knife!" Penn cried. "To cut us free while the dog distracts him."

But Llynn had fury of her own. She grabbed at the man, seeking an opening for her knee. He turned on her, throwing her to the floor with one arm.

"Get him!" Lloyd cried, and Obsidian obeyed. She let go of the man's arm and scrambled to reach his throat. Meanwhile Llynn scrambled back to her feet and came at him again, nails first. This was folly; she would have been much better off dashing for a knife. But it had more effect than it deserved.

Probably the man could have handled them both. But the double attack had caught him by surprise. He backed away, then turned and lunged for the front door. He jerked it open and wedged out.

"Enough!" Lloyd called. Dog and girl desisted, letting the man go.

"Get the setting!" Penn said.

Llynn slapped her hand against the panel, changing the setting randomly. Now they were safe from the man.

After that it was a matter of unwinding. Chandelle got a kitchen knife and cut Penn and Lloyd free. Penn checked the front and back doors, making sure that neither had any threats. Llynn kissed Lloyd on the nose. Lloyd hugged Obsidian. They were all phenomenally relieved to have escaped more serious consequences.

There was a groan. All of them went silent. They had forgotten the fugitive man—and now he was reviving.

What were they going to do with him?

Chapter 7
Kailash

Llynn stared at the injured man. Now she saw what she had not noticed in the press of action: he was of Asiatic complexion. That suggested that he was not a local Moscow resident. He could be a visitor, perhaps on business.

His shirt was soaking with blood. She didn't know how badly injured he was, but it must be serious, because he had passed out once he entered the house. He had missed most of the action, which was maybe just as well.

He groaned again, and tried to sit up. "No, no, lie down, relax," she said soothingly. "You're safe now."

Then Chandelle was there with bandages and a basin of water. "Get his shirt off," she said. "We must find out the extent of his injury."

Llynn put her hands to the man's shirt. He tried to protest, but she smiled, cautioning him, and he relaxed. On one level she found this pleasant: her ability as a woman to pacify a hurting man. It was a gender role she had not adopted before, but now she liked it. It didn't hurt that the man was young—perhaps twenty—and clean cut.

They worked his shirt open, spreading it on the floor to either side. The wound was laid out to view: a slice across the right ribs and into the flesh below. "It was a slashing cut," Chandelle said. "The ribs deflected it, but not enough. It's not deep; his problem is mainly loss of blood. We'll have to clean it and bandage it to halt the bleeding. Then he will have to rest until he heals."

"I'll take care of him," Llynn said. "It's my fault he's here."

"I think he would be dead by now if you hadn't brought him

in."

"I guess so. When I saw him being chased like that, I just had to do something."

Penn spoke from across the room. "You realize, of course, that he is a stranger. We don't know him or his motives. This compromises our occupancy of this house."

"I know, and I'm sorry," Llynn said. "I'm a foolish girl. But we can put him back in Moscow when the coast is clear."

Chandelle washed the man's side, then touched his hand. "I must clean the wound," she said. "It will hurt." Then, to Llynn: "Hold his hand."

"His hand?"

"So he doesn't get in the way."

Llynn took the man's right hand in both of hers. "We have to do this," she said, knowing he didn't understand.

Chandelle dabbed at the wound. The man flinched. His arm flexed, his hand clenching.

"No, no!" Llynn said, hanging on. His arm was not unduly muscular, and he was weak from injury, so she was able to keep it captive. "You must let us clean it."

He relaxed. Then Chandelle dabbed again, trying to clear the partly coagulated blood. The man tensed, and gasped with pain, trying to protect it with his hand.

"No," Llynn repeated. She drew his forearm in toward her, trying to hold it firmly.

Chandelle dabbed a third time. This time Llynn anticipated the man's reaction, and hugged his hand to her chest.

After that, he tensed when Chandelle's cleaning hurt him, but did not try to move his arm. Llynn realized that he must be aware of her bosom, slight as it was, and satisfied to remain as he was. She hadn't intended to vamp him, but on the other hand it was further evidence of her femininity, and she found that she rather liked making it count. So long as no one could accuse her of being forward.

"It's clean," Chandelle said. "Now the antiseptic. This will really hurt, for a moment."

Llynn spoke to the man. "Medicine," she said. "Clean the wound. Hurt." She made a hiss of intaken breath through her teeth. "Understand?"

He turned his head and looked at her directly for the first time. His eyes were brown. He nodded slightly.

She clutched his hand more tightly, prepared to hand on when he reacted to the new pain. "Now," she said.

Chandelle applied the antiseptic. The man's whole body stiffened, except for his arm. Maybe that was the one part of him that felt no pain.

In due course Chandelle finished, and put a dressing on the wound, and a bandage on the dressing. Llynn noted her grandmother's competence with a certain muted pride; it was her business to know what to do when someone was hurt, and she was good at it. "This should be all right, if he doesn't get too active. I'll have to change it every so often, but it shouldn't bother him between times."

"All done," Llynn said to the man, and released his hand.

His head turned to her again, and he smiled. He was halfway handsome when he did that.

"Now he should eat something," Chandelle said. "He needs nourishment to recover. And rest, of course. I'll go fix some soup."

"Where's he going to stay?" Lloyd asked.

Llynn hadn't thought of that. "I guess he can have my room, since I'm responsible for him being here. I'll sleep on the couch in the living room."

"No," Penn said firmly. "*He'll* sleep on the couch. You will sleep in your own room—and lock the door."

Llynn opened her mouth to protest, then remembered how the brute of a thug had ripped open her shirt and pawed her bra. *Any* strange man could be dangerous. All they knew about this one was that he had been fleeing attackers, and was wounded.

He could be a criminal, maybe a deserter from a gang. So they did have to be careful. Just as Grandma was competent in caregiving, Grandpa was competent in protection. "Yes."

"But for now, we'll try to make him comfortable where he is, on the floor," Penn said.

Chandelle arrived with a bowl of hot soup on an elevated bed tray. She brought it close enough to the man's face for him to see and smell it. He smiled, knowing food when he saw it.

"We'll have to help him to sit up," Penn said. "Take his left shoulder, Llynn."

Llynn obeyed with alacrity. She knew that Penn was giving her the left side, because his greater strength would be needed on the right side, to prevent aggravation to the wound.

They lifted and hauled, and got the man into a sitting position, though he did groan with pain as his midsection flexed. They used pillows to prop him up against the wall. Chandelle put the tray over his legs. Then he tried to pick up the spoon with his right hand—and almost knocked over the soup. The pain of that side made it unsteady.

"I'll help," Llynn said. She took the spoon, dipped it into the bowl, waited for it to cool sufficiently, then put it to the man's mouth. He looked a bit askance at this, but she smiled at him, and he opened his mouth. This, too, was fun, in its novelty; maybe she was cut out to be a nurse.

While she fed the man, the grandparents went to another room. Lloyd, evidently on orders, remained in the living room, and so did Obsidian. Maybe that was just as well. Why take chances with a stranger who might not be as weak as he seemed?

The job was slow, but they got through the soup. Chandelle brought a glass of water, and Llynn steadied the man's hand with her own while he drank. Very little spilled. They were a success.

Chandelle brought blankets, pillows, and a sleeping bag, forming a bed. She also brought a change of clothing, having evidently judged the man's size and found something close enough in a closet. This house always had something close enough. "Penn, take him to the downstairs bathroom," she said as she took away the bed tray.

Llynn nodded. Naturally the man had natural functions, and he wouldn't want a girl helping him change clothing.

Penn kneeled beside the man. "Bathroom," he said. "Wash." He made washing motions. "Pee." He touched his crotch. "Change." He showed the clean clothes.

The man nodded. It would have been hard to misunderstand such an explanation.

They heaved on the man's shoulders and got him to his feet. They walked him to the bathroom. Llynn grabbed Obsidian, who wanted to go too. The dog liked to be in the middle of any activity of any nature, and tended to be jealous of attention paid to others. Then Penn took him on in, while Llynn retreated. She did not want to get involved in this.

"You know this is temporary," Lloyd told her. "We can't keep him."

"I know," she said, rubbing the dog's ears. "But I think we did right to save him from those thugs. Otherwise he would have been dead."

"Yeah. But who is he? Maybe he's a thug himself."

"He couldn't be. He looks nothing like a criminal."

"That's girl talk! *I* could be a criminal."

She eyed him appraisingly. "That's no refutation. You do look the part."

He laughed. "Walked into that one. But the point is—"

"I know. And you're right. We do have to be careful."

"We can't even talk with him. We don't know anything about him."

Chandelle appeared. "I have an idea. Maybe we *can* talk with him."

"You know Russian, Grandma?" the boy asked.

"No. But maybe the house does."

"The house?" Llynn asked blankly.

"Those artifacts in the attic. That one that's like the hearing aid, except that it doesn't work. We never tried it on a different language."

"A different language!" Llynn echoed. "That just might be it! How can it translate, if there's nothing to translate? But now there is."

They hurried to the attic, Obsidian leading the way, and fetched the earpiece in question. "Do you want to try it?" Chandelle inquired.

"Yes!" Llynn put on the unit.

"But if it works, how do you know for what language?" Lloyd asked.

They hadn't thought of that. The thing could be a perfect translator—and do them no good at all. There seemed to be no control, no way to set it.

"But you know," Lloyd said, answering his own question, "this house has a way of making things work, when you use them right. So maybe it knows what it's doing."

Llynn hoped so. She didn't relish trying to learn Russian.

They returned to the living room. The man was now in the new clothing, and sitting on the couch. He looked much better. Penn had even combed his hair.

"Say something," Llynn said to the man.

He looked at her, not understanding.

"Speak," she said. She put her hand to her mouth, like a megaphone. "Say anything."

"You want me to speak?" the man asked. The quality was different, but the words made sense: she was understanding the foreign language.

"It works!" Llynn almost screamed.

All of them looked at her, including the dog, not understanding for their separate reasons.

She took off the earpiece and approached the man. "Let me

put this on you," she said. "Maybe it will make you understand us."

He sat still while she fitted the earpiece to his ear. Then she stood back and spoke. "Now do you understand me?"

The man jumped, then winced as his side hurt. He spoke a rapid stream of words. Obsidian jumped to her feet, thinking there was a problem.

"Oops," Llynn said. "It works—but we need two of them."

"There are others there," Chandelle said. "Enough for us all." She disappeared, Obsidian following her. A person in motion was always more interesting than one in place.

"It's a most accommodating house," Penn remarked. "It has whatever we need, in the quantity we need, once we realize *what* we need."

"But it sure makes us work to realize," Lloyd said.

The man looked around, evidently understanding the words but not their context.

Llynn spoke carefully to him. "It is a translator," she said. "We will fetch more of them, so we can understand you. Right now we can't."

The man nodded. He touched his ear, appreciating the wonder of the earpiece.

Soon Chandelle returned with four more earpieces. Each of them donned one. And suddenly the language barrier was gone.

"My salutation," the man said.

"Who are you?" Penn asked. "Why were you being chased by those men?"

"I am Kailash, from Kashmir."

"India or Pakistan?" Penn asked. "The region is contested."

Llynn hadn't known that. But then geography had never been her strong point.

"The Himalayas of India," the man said. "I came to Moscow to try to find my sister Shree. But when I inquired, they attacked me. I managed to get away, but they pursued me. I almost escaped by fleeing into a quiet residential section, but they found me."

They questioned him, and the rest of the story came clear. Kailash was twenty, a hopeful artist, but in the backwoods mountain region the best such work he could find was painting designs on crockery intended for the tourist trade. Times were hard, for there had been warfare there recently, and things were changing even in the outlying regions, making them harder.

His sister Shree was eighteen, and beautiful. She had trained to be a secretary, for she was good with language and writing. She and Kailash had enjoyed debating each other, just for the pleasure of word play. But there was little need locally for such employment. So she had answered an ad for an excellent job in Delhi, more than three hundred miles away. The pay was far better than anything in the mountains, and she hoped to send money back to support the family.

But no money had come back. In fact Shree disappeared. Alarmed, Kailash had gathered what little money and equipment he had, and gone to investigate. He had to work at whatever he could find to support himself on the way, and that made the search difficult, but he had learned that the job Shree had gone to was actually foreign, in Moscow. She had gone there, though it was surprising that she hadn't sent word to her family about it. But he hadn't found her at the given Moscow address. Then the thugs had come after him. He assumed it was because he was an obvious foreigner, so was easy prey.

"I doubt it," Penn said.

"It is the truth!" Kailash protested. "I swear!"

"I wasn't doubting you," Penn said. "I was doubting that the thugs were merely picking easy prey."

Llynn was perplexed. "But why else would they go after him, when he was just inquiring?"

"White slavery," Penn said. "It's big business, especially in the defunct Soviet Union. Young women are promised excellent jobs in distant cities, but are instead sold into prostitution."

"Prostitution!" Kailash exclaimed in horror. "That can't be!"

"It's not voluntary on their part," Penn said. "They have no choice. Their papers are taken, so they are stranded as aliens, often not even speaking the local language. They are rendered completely dependent on the pimps, who are ruthlessly cruel. The women must oblige, or be beaten, or tortured in ways that don't show."

"But Shree is an innocent girl! She could never—"

"They prefer innocence. Innocents are easier to cow, and free of disease. Is she pretty?"

"Yes, very much so. But—"

"Let's hope there is some other explanation," Chandelle said. But she did not look confident.

"I must find her," Kailash said. "I must bring her home."

"Not before you recover," Chandelle said. "You can't go back out on the street in this condition."

Kailash touched his injured side. "I can't," he agreed. "But if Shree is in danger of—of—"

"We have to help him," Llynn said.

But Penn looked doubtful. "It isn't that simple."

"Yes it is," she protested hotly. "You wouldn't let *me* be taken like that. Why let his sister?"

"I can answer that," Kailash said sadly. "The four of you have been most generous to me, and I think saved my life. But you have business of your own, and I am interfering."

"That, too," Penn agreed.

"There's something else?" Llynn demanded.

"And I am a stranger," Kailash said. "How can you believe what I say?"

Penn nodded. "You have a good grasp of the situation."

"But why should we doubt him?" Llynn asked.

Kailash answered again. "I could be telling you a story to encourage your trust, and then rob you and sneak away."

"No you couldn't."

"But you can't be sure. I trust you because you saved my life and have not robbed me. But you can't trust me."

"You can't sneak away," Llynn said. "Because—"

"Ixnay," Lloyd said.

She realized that she had been about to give away the secret of the door. They were right: they could not afford to trust a stranger. "Anyway, you need to rest and recover. So it doesn't matter."

"I think I am being in the way," Kailash said. "I can not repay you for your help and kindness to me, but I can relieve you of the burden of my presence. If you will take me to the Indian embassy—"

"No," she said.

"What, you're sweet on him?" Lloyd asked insolently.

"No! It's just—"

Penn and Chandelle exchanged a look. "You stay with Kailash," Penn said. "We'll see what we can do."

"There is no need to attend to me," Kailash said. "I will merely sleep."

"Nevertheless, we must watch you, until we can be sure of you," Penn said.

"Oh. Yes. Of course."

Llynn was disgusted, but the truth was she was intrigued by this polite young man. "Okay, I'll stay. Mind if I watch TV?"

"It is not my place to object."

So she turned on the set, while the others left the room. Obsidian hesitated, then decided that there was more of interest in the living room, and stayed. She lay down beside the couch.

The program came on in English. Then Llynn thought of something. "I wonder if this has an Indian version?"

"We do have television in our village," Kailash said. "We are not entirely primitive."

"This is special." She invoked the special controls. Sure enough:

there was a table for different languages. She selected India—and was rewarded by a subset of many languages she had never heard of. "Which one's yours?" she asked.

"My native language? But your excellent translation device makes that unnecessary."

"Still, I'd like to see if this works."

He guided her to one of the languages, and she invoked it. But the TV continued speaking in English. "It's not working."

"Oh, but it is," Kailash said. "Remove your translator."

"Oh." She did so. Suddenly she understood none of the dialogue. She saw that Kailash had removed his own ear unit. He was watching and listening, and nodding: he understood it.

He said something, but she could not understand. She put her unit back on. "What was that?"

Kailash smiled, though he could not have understood her words, except by context. "I understand the television perfectly. It is indeed in my language. This is remarkable."

"It's a remarkable set," she said.

"It is a remarkable house."

She realized that some of the secrets of the house had already been revealed. "Yes."

He returned the unit to his ear. "If I may inquire—"

How much could she tell him? "I don't know."

"I do not wish to impose, but your presence diverts me from my discomfort, and I would like to talk."

Her presence diverted him? She liked that too. "Yes, sure."

"It is not possible to avoid the realization that this is no ordinary domicile. You seem to be ordinary people from America, no offense, and I am from a primitive village, but I have never heard of technology like this." He indicated the earpiece. "And I saw that the scene beyond the door changed in a manner I thought it could not. You surely have excellent reason to say that I could not simply walk out."

He was observant. In fact, he was no fool. She liked that. She would have to tell him something. “Yes. Moscow is not there anymore.”

“But how could this be?”

“How can I tell you, if I can’t trust you?”

He spread his hands. “I apologize. I should not ask. I will simply accept that this is a magic house.”

So she told him. “Not magic, exactly. Super science. This house can travel. We started in America, and went to other cities, and stopped in Moscow. We happened to be there when you came, so we helped you.”

“You made them help me.”

Llynn felt herself blushing. “I guess I did. But I couldn’t just let three men murder you.”

“I owe you my life, whatever your motive. It was an extremely fortunate coincidence that brought me to your location at that time.”

“I guess so,” she agreed uncomfortably. Obsidian, recognizing that she was troubled, lifted her head sympathetically.

“Do you believe in divine guidance?”

“No.”

“I do. I think that what you would call fate guided my steps, and put me where I could be saved.”

“It was just chance. You could have taken a hundred other streets.”

“Yes. But I did not. And so I was saved, when I should have perished. By a house that I think can not exist.”

That made her wonder. He was right about the coincidence: it was really too much to be believed. Could the house have had a purpose?

“I’m going to have to tell you more,” she said. “It’s an alien house. We’re just using it for a month. We don’t know who built it.”

“Fate built it. And brought it here, to save me.”

Llynn shook her head. “I don’t want to offend you, but I’m not much on eastern religion or whatever. I don't think the house cares about you. Or us. It's just a very advanced alien residence."

"And I do not wish to offend you, Llynn. I may call you that?"

"Sure." She liked to hear him say her name. It had a different quality, with his translated accent.

"But I do disagree. Let us accept the fact that we differ in belief, and see if we can't find some common ground. Will you consider my thesis?"

"That you were guided here? Okay, for now. But we weren't guided to you, so it's still a wild coincidence that we should be there right when you needed us."

"Perhaps. You say you do not know who made the house. How then can you say what its purpose is?"

"I guess I can't," she admitted.

"Could you entertain the notion that perhaps the house seeks people? People suitable to occupy it? That just as people need houses, houses need people, or they are unfulfilled?"

Llynn glanced quickly at him. This guy was disturbingly sharp. "I suppose."

"Or that perhaps those who made the house wanted it to be occupied by people who would appreciate it. Perhaps it is designed to discourage those who are unsuitable."

"Yes!" she exclaimed. "Grandpa says that lots of people looked at it, and wouldn't take it. Because of the back door."

"The back door?"

"It—oh, hell, you'll figure it out anyway. It opens on a forest. Sometimes. It has different settings."

He raised a finger. "The men who pursued me—did they not come into the house? Where did they go?"

"Out the back," she said. "And we changed the setting. So they're gone."

"You isolated them in some other region?"

"Yes. And the third one we drove out the front door, and changed *that* setting, so he's in Moscow, but we aren't."

Kailash nodded. "Why would a forest frighten people?"

"Because it surrounds the house. Even though the house is in a city. It—it's hard to explain. But it scares people, because there's no place for a big forest in the middle of a city."

"The world of the back door is different from the world of the front door?"

"Yes. The doors are—are portals to other places. And they don't have to match. It's weird."

"I will not say I understand perfectly, but I can appreciate how such a thing could seem unsettling. Why didn't it unsettle you?"

"It did. But I loved it. It's like playing in the fifth dimension. A real challenge. I guess Grandpa and Grandma saw it the same way. And it *is* a really nice house. It has things for all of us."

"Like the translation units?"

"Yes. And the TV. And fabulous access to the Internet. And even clothes and food we like."

"Then I think you have made my case. This house desires you, so it makes itself appealing to you. And not to others. It must see something in you that it likes."

"I guess so," Lynn said, feeling awed. The house *did* want them.

Obsidian nuzzled her hand. "And you too," she said to the dog. "I'm sure it wants you."

"So it is not coincidence that you occupy it. Many looked, but only your family stayed. Could it also desire me?"

"I guess," she agreed, her awe at the concept continuing. "But it was sheer chance that you came by, right when we happened to be in Moscow."

"That I wish to address. Assume that the house is aware of people, and recognizes those with attributes it desires. It took you in, and that is good. But it needs more people. So when it saw me, it desired me, and took me in too."

"Could be. But if you hadn't come by just when—"

"Yes. Such coincidence makes me nervous, especially since it was my life at issue. But could it have been aware of me when you were not in Moscow?"

"How can it be aware of anything, when it isn't there? There's just a—an empty block, when the house is away."

"How do you know?"

"We tried to get in. That's what we were doing, when you came by. There was nothing there—just a closed off block."

"You could not enter it?"

"Right. It's impervious."

"Then how can you say there is nothing inside?"

She paused. "I—I guess I can't. But—"

"Such as perhaps a unit that senses people, suitable and unsuitable."

"I guess there could be. But what good can that do, when we're not there?"

"I mean no offense. But could the house influence you?"

"What, mind control? I don't think so."

Kailash frowned. "The spirits can be subtle. I think of this house as a spirit, for convenience. Perhaps it could not, or would not, influence you directly. But indirectly, such as by providing things you appreciate, such as versatile television—"

"Agreed. Indirectly, there's a lot."

"And if you wished to experiment with cities, and selected randomly, could it make the choice for you?"

"Grandpa pushed the buttons. Grandpa chose the city."

"But if he did not care which city—could the house cause him to choose Moscow?"

She stared at him. "Maybe so."

"So if it sensed me in Moscow, and desired my entry, could it then bring you to Moscow to intercept me?"

Her head was whirling. "I—I guess it could."

"I do not mean to cause you distress. But as I reflect, I remember something I did not credit at first. When I came to Moscow, and passed this neighborhood on my way to inquire for my sister, I felt an odd temptation. I wished to go in a certain direction.

But that was not where I needed to go, so I overrode it and went about my business. But when I fled, hardly caring where I went, this is the direction I came. Toward this house."

"It summoned you!" she exclaimed. "It reeled you in—when it could. And it brought us in, the same time, so we could connect. So we could save you. Suddenly it makes sense!"

Kailash leaned back, carefully. "Of course this is merely conjecture."

"Don't back off now!" she flared. "You've convinced me."

"And me," Penn said, entering the room, and the dog jumped up to greet him. "It eliminates coincidence almost entirely."

"You were listening?" Llynn asked, embarrassed for no reason she could fathom at the moment.

"I was returning, and heard you talking, and paused," Penn said. "It was so interesting that I didn't want to interrupt."

"I see things in a manner you may not," Kailash said delicately.

"No, I think you could be right. I don't like coincidence any better than you do. It explains a great deal. I think we had better bring you in on the remaining secrets of the house."

"But we don't know that we can trust him," Llynn said, though she did trust him now.

"That's next," Penn said. "We found what we were looking for, thanks to Chandelle's expertise with the squiggle script." He held up an open bracelet. "Put this on, Llynn."

She did, bemused. "What's this, a dingus that stops lying?"

"Not exactly. Try telling a lie."

"My name is the Queen of Sheba." She paused. "No reaction."

"My name is the King of Sheba," Penn said.

Llynn jumped. The band had tingled. "It told me *you* lied," she said.

"Yes. It seems to be ideal. It lets you lie, while warning you about the lies of others."

"This is great! Now we can verify Kailash." She turned to the man. "Tell me a lie."

"I think you are ugly."

The bracelet tingled. Llynn felt herself blushing again. "Tell me another."

"Everything I told you about my personal history is false."

The bracelet tingled. "That's a lie," Llynn said. "Which means what you said must be true."

"Not necessarily," Kailash said. "Some of what I told you might be true, and some false. So it would be a lie that all of it is false, but would nevertheless deceive you."

She looked at Penn. "Grandpa, this man is too smart for me." But she liked the man's evident intelligence, and his compliment.

"Are you deceiving us?" Penn asked Kailash.

"No."

The bracelet did not tingle. "He's not lying," she said.

"Can we trust you?" Penn asked.

"Yes. I am grateful for the way you saved my life, and will return the favor if I can."

"No tingle," Llynn said.

Penn tried once more. "Do you have designs on Llynn?"

"Grandpa!" she cried, blushing again.

So did Kailash, though it showed less on his darker skin. "I hardly know her."

The bracelet tingled. Llynn held it up, signaling that she had felt it. The man had been evasive, and the bracelet interpreted that as a lie.

"Do you mean her any harm?" Penn asked.

"No!"

No tingle.

"But you do like her."

"Yes."

"Can we stop this now?" Llynn asked, mortified.

"I find her attractive," Kailash said. "She has been kind to me, and attentive, and she is pretty. I react as any man would. But I mean her no harm, and will not pursue her. I realize she is young, though in my culture she would be of age. I regret causing distress."

Penn nodded. "He finds you appealing. Do you object, Llynn?"

"Yes!" But she flinched, expecting the bracelet to tingle, despite knowing better. "No."

"I think we have done enough for now," Penn said. "Kailash must rest. But tomorrow I suggest that the two of you experiment with the truth band, and ascertain its limitations. We may have good use for it, in due course."

Kailash nodded. "I shall be glad to cooperate."

Llynn hesitated. "Promise you won't ask that question of me, when you have the bracelet. About my feelings."

"I give you my oath," Kailash said, and the band did not tingle.

But Llynn wasn't sure she was relieved. She was flattered by his attention, and did like him, and she knew it showed. He hardly needed to ask.

Chapter 8
Shree

Lloyd paused as he passed the plaque by the stairway. "Hey—it's up to number eight!" he exclaimed. "We made another step."

"Maybe it was the lie detector," Penn said.

"Well, it didn't budge for the hearing aid, or the translator, so why should it for the lie detector?"

"Good point. It moved to 7 when Chandelle deciphered the squiggle print, and not for the subsequent results of that. So what did we do this time?"

"Beats me, Grandpa."

"Maybe Chandelle will know."

They went to the kitchen, where Chandelle was happily working. "The plaque has advanced, but we aren't sure why," Penn said.

"For realizing that the house summons its residents," she said promptly. "Kailash figured that out."

Penn and Lloyd exchanged a glance, and then a shrug. She was probably right. The plaque seemed to react to the grasping of principles more than to details.

Lloyd went on to the living room. Kailash and Llynn and Obsidian were there, working on the ramifications of the lie detector. It was clear that she was getting sweet on him, and he rather liked her. The grandparents made no objection, probably because they thought Kailash was a better prospect than that gang leader she had gone with before. Lloyd tried to suppress a surge of jealousy. He was only thirteen, but he did know what girls were for, and wished he had one of his own. But no girl he had ever thought of liking had ever had any interest in him. Girls wanted men, and he was a boy. A mouthy boy.

"How's it going?" he asked.

"We've pretty well figured out the nuances of the lie band," Llynn said. "But we're thinking that if we want to rescue Kailash's sister Shree, we'll need more than that and the translators."

"You'll need a gun," Lloyd said.

"Guns are dangerous," Kailash said. "They are instruments of war." He didn't like war, as he had explained, because of the fighting that had gone on in his neighborhood, as India and Pakistan tried to take over Kashmir. He hadn't said so, but Lloyd suspected that members of Kailash's family had been shot. Lloyd didn't know much about Buddhism or Hinduism or whatever it was, but gathered they didn't much like violence.

"We're wondering whether there's something in the attic," Lynn said. "Maybe not a gun, but something better."

"I'll ask Grandma," Lloyd said. He returned to the kitchen and explained their concern.

"The problem with guns is that they can be as deadly to their owners as to others," Penn said. "That's why they are kept under lock, in the military, when not in use, and the ammunition locked elsewhere. It would be better to find the perfect defense."

"Yes," Chandelle agreed. "Something that can only safeguard, not threaten. I will check the squiggles."

"So are we going to rescue his sister?" Lloyd asked.

Penn and Chandelle exchanged a glance. "I suppose we are going to try," Penn said. "Llynn will insist."

"Yeah. She's sweet on him."

"He is an impressive young man, very intelligent," Chandelle said. "Yet no doubt he will return home, once he recovers his sister."

"What about the way the house brings in the people it wants?" Lloyd asked. "Why would it let him go?"

The grandparents exchanged another glance. "Do you think the house can hold a person who doesn't wish to be held?" Chandelle asked.

"Sure. By making him want to be held. Like it made us."

Penn frowned. "Do you feel we are captives of the house?"

"Naw. It just makes us want it, like—like a girl making a man want her."

"By providing us with substance for our dreams," Penn agreed. "For you, it's that powerful Internet connection."

"Sure." But it wasn't enough, Lloyd thought. The house couldn't give him a girl. That was just too complicated, considering what it had to work with. So all he could do was maintain his usual front of girl-hating. He wasn't fooling Llynn, but it would do for the others.

"I think we are indeed committed," Chandelle said. "We can't let his sister be victim of white slavers. But you are right: we will need more than we have at present."

"First we'll need to find her," Penn said. "I have no idea how to proceed with that."

"I do," Lloyd said. "I can do a query on the Internet. Sure, I know it won't be any good to ask for her by name, but I can pretend to be a guy looking for a doll, and make sure she fits the description, and maybe I'll get a bite."

Chandelle faced away. "I think I do not wish to inquire about this process," she said.

But Penn was interested. "You can do this? You can emulate an older male?"

"Sure. I do it all the time, online. 'Cause I don't like what I am, so I make a better persona. Everyone on the Net knows it's fake, but they don't know for sure it's just a kid behind it. It could be a horny old man."

"Then question Kailash about his sister," Penn said. "So you know exactly what you are looking for. If you can make this work, it will greatly facilitate things."

"His sister," Lloyd echoed glumly. Looking for a sister, any sister, was not the stuff of dreams. But what choice did he have? He was the only one who could do the search. And there was a current of interest, because Kailash had said she was lovely.

So he returned to the living room. "I gotta learn all about your sister, so I can do an Internet search for her," he told Kailash.

Llynn laughed. "Who says there's no such thing as hell on earth? Lloyd has to study a woman."

"Shut up," he said without force. She did like teasing him, knowing the falsity of his stance.

"I can't get over this demonstration of divine justice," she said, pushing it. "Lloyd rescuing a *gurrl.*"

Kailash looked slightly pained. "My sister Shree is very nice. You would surely like her if you knew her."

An eighteen year old secretary? She would see him as the juvenile snot he was. "Well, anyway, I gotta know enough about her so I can describe her accurately, and maybe run her down that way. Without letting anybody catch on that I'm not a john."

"But of course you're not John. Your name is Lloyd."

Llynn smiled. "There are some idioms the translation doesn't clarify. A john is a man who patronizes prosti—" She broke off, remembering that Kailash couldn't stand to think of his sister that way.

"A john is a jerk," Lloyd said. "That much I can do."

Kailash paused. Then he reconciled himself. "Perhaps so. My description is colored by my love for her, but I sincerely believe that she is a very fine person. I will try to describe her accurately. Will you need to make notes?"

"Naw. I can remember."

"There is a fair amount of detail. Perhaps—"

Llynn cut in. "Lloyd's got close to eidetic memory. He's a snot, but he's a *smart* snot. He doesn't need notes."

"Thanks so much for that recommendation, cousin Llynnburger," Lloyd said.

"What is that term?" Kailash asked, perplexed.

"It's a stupid pun," Llynn said, grimacing. "Limburger cheese smells really strong."

"In fact it stinks," Lloyd added.

Kailash considered. "I hear you in my own language, so per-aps the nuances are lost in translation. But I do know of imburger cheese, and Llynnburger—oh, I see!" He burst out aughing.

Llynn tried to hold her scowl, but had to start laughing with im. Lloyd found himself liking the man; his laugh was genu-ne.

They got down to the description. "She is about two inches elow Llynn's height," Kailash said. "Long dark hair, brown eyes, ark complexion like mine. Her face is almond shaped, and ather pretty, except perhaps for the small mole just above her eft eyebrow. Her body is svelte, yet fuller than Llynn's; she is a vell developed woman."

He continued the description, and Lloyd set it in his memory. picture was forming of a girl with a cute face and nice figure, wo inches shorter than he was. Sure she was five years older; till, he could admire her in his imagination, like a pin-up girl.

Kailash told of Shree's personality quirks, and these too be-ame part of the picture. He told of childhood misadventures, howing the way she reacted to joy and stress and boredom. Lloyd istened, and his picture of her deepened. This was an ideal voman, but for her age and culture. But also exactly the kind vho would not even see him on the street.

Finally the description was complete. "I'll start the search," he aid. "It may take a while, if it even works."

"I understand," Kailash said. "I sincerely appreciate your ef-ort."

Lloyd went to the computer cubby and got online. First he had o establish his persona: Louie, age 23, rich, horny, with special-zed tastes. He set up an online bank account, discovering to his urprise that the house actually had online funds he could draw n. He instituted a paper trail, for all that none of it was on pa-er, showing Louie's prior participation on the Internet. Louie liked sexy chatrooms, and porno shops, and phone sex, and he didn't much care about expense. Only when he had an identity that would stand up to inspection by anyone who was less adept at hacking than he, Lloyd, was, did he start using it. "I'm tired of the usual floozies," he typed. "I want something different."

Then he set up a search. The porno and procurement aspects of the Internet were actually only a tiny part of it, less than one per cent, but they drew a lot of business. He had not before dared to view straight porno sites, but now Louie did. They thrilled him unmercifully, but he pretended indifference. "None of these cows," he typed. "I want something more slender, without being thin. Maybe five two, B-cup bra, dark brown hair, heart shaped face—no, make that almond shaped. A perfect beauty—no, let's have an imperfection, like a scar—no, that's a turn-off; make it a mole, not too big." He continued, gradually forming the description of Shree, as if by sheer chance.

There were takers. Different online pimps put pictures on. Pictures—

"Hey, Kailash!" he called. "Can you get over here? It's important."

Kailash came to the cubby, supported by Llynn. "You have found her?" he asked hopefully.

"Not yet. But check these pictures. Is any her?"

Kailash looked. "No, no," he said, checking one and another. "No—wait, perhaps, if her hair were cut short and changed. Her eyebrow—can we see that closer?"

Lloyd magnified the picture, orienting on the left brow. There, almost concealed by bangs, was a mole.

"This is Shree!" Kailash said. "Where is she?"

"In Riyadh, Saudi Arabia," Lloyd said. "You know she's a—they made her—"

"I know," Kailash said heavily. "I must rescue her."

"I can make an appointment for Louie to be with her, for a good price. But how to get her out of there I don't know. It's not like a Sunday walk in the park."

"There must be a way."

"So what's the date?"

"Make it in three days," Llynn said. "We'll be ready by then—or else."

So Louie made a date with Shree for three days hence, and transferred a hefty binder fee. Then he moved on through the Net, checking other sites, so that if anyone were tracing him, he wouldn't suspiciously disappear. Lloyd would have to animate him in the intervening days, too, to keep up appearances. Just in case.

Then he exited and went to see what else was happening in the house. Chandelle was poring over pages of copied squiggles, while Penn was lining up assorted devices from the attic. Llynn was in the living room talking with Kailash, who was animated by the discovery of his sister.

Lloyd joined the grandparents. "So have you found a gun?"

"No gun," Penn said. "But two prospects." He indicated a large white band, and a similar black band on the table. "They seem to surround the users in some way, but we haven't found out how."

"The squiggles don't tell you?"

"Here they are," Chandelle said, showing him a page. "I can read them, but they don't clarify enough. The bands are worn like belts, around the waist. Something scintillates around the person. But when we actually try them, nothing happens."

"Like the translator, huh?"

"Like that, yes," Penn agreed. "We're sure there is a key, that will be obvious in retrospect, but so far it eludes us."

"Maybe I can figure it out," Lloyd said. "Which one do I try?"

Penn shrugged. "We would like to solve either. Preferably both."

Lloyd picked up the black band. "How do I put it on?"

"You have to step into it, or don it over your head. It will stretch to accommodate your motions."

Lloyd tried it. Sure enough, the band was like thick rubber, and he had no trouble passing it over his head. When it reached his waist, it cinched in snug but not tight. It was really quite comfortable.

"You figure this protects me?" he asked.

"The symbols suggest that it does," Chandelle said. "But they don't say how."

"What did you try, that you might need protection from?"

Penn shrugged. "We couldn't think how to test it, until we know how it works."

"Catch 22. I gotta face something dangerous."

"We don't want anyone risking injury," Chandelle said.

"Maybe pretend it. Grandpa, come at me with a knife, like you mean it."

Penn shrugged. He brought out his penknife. He lifted it, and charged Lloyd. And sheered off, well clear of any flesh.

"You gotta make it more realistic than that," Lloyd said.

"I tried," Penn said. "Something pushed me away."

"Then maybe we got something." Lloyd pondered briefly, then laid his hand on the table. "Stab me. Not for real. I mean, you know."

"I know. Don't move your hand." Penn lifted the knife, then brought it forcefully down. It plunged into the table, not even close.

"That doesn't prove anything," Lloyd said. "You should miss by an inch, not a foot."

"I tried," Penn repeated. "Let me try it again."

This time he moved the knife more slowly. It came down about three inches from Lloyd's hand. "There is definitely a force. The more force I apply, the more it pushes me away."

"Let me try," Lloyd said. He reached across and took the knife from Penn's hand. He plunged it down just beyond his grandfather's fingers. "I didn't feel any push."

"As with the lie detector," Penn said. "It doesn't restrict the wearer. But it affects his input."

"I guess. But suppose you held the knife, and I walked into it? I mean if I was running, and you stood there and let me impale myself? Then the belt wouldn't protect me."

Penn stroked his chin. "Good point. Try slamming your fist into the table."

Lloyd tried it. His hand struck the table, but not with much force. He tried again, and it was as if it passed through a cushion before reaching the hard surface. "It's shielding me," he said. "I can't hit the table hard."

Penn nodded. "This is becoming more interesting. I think we need a sterner test."

"Don't try anything dangerous," Chandelle cautioned them, alarmed.

"Maybe the belt works when it's not on a person," Lloyd said. "So we could really give it the works."

"Good idea. Let's see if we can damage it, by itself."

Lloyd removed the belt and set it on the table. Penn went to the garage and got a heavy wrench. He struck hard at the belt—and couldn't hit it. "But would it stop a bullet?" he asked.

Lloyd fetched a kitchen knife and tried to stab the belt. It turned his blade aside. The harder he tried, the worse he missed it. "I don't think a bullet would get anywhere close. It pushes back as hard as something comes at it."

"So it seems. Still, its protection can hardly be complete. Suppose the wearer fell in a well?"

"Let me put it on and try jumping off the table," Lloyd said.

"Not off the kitchen table," Chandelle protested.

"Off the outer steps," Penn said quickly.

Lloyd donned the best, and they went out the back door. It remained set where Chandelle had left it, at the alien village. By common consent, they had not returned it to the original forest, where the thugs had been stranded.

Lloyd stood on the top step, and jumped off. He braced for the landing three feet below, but it was cushioned. He turned and kicked the steps, but that too was buffered. He went back to the top and jumped off, lifting his feet to land on his rear. There was no pain. It was like landing on jelly.

"I can't hurt myself," he said.

"So I see. It is a shield against any forcefully approaching object. To it, the ground is approaching your body, so it pads you. I believe it would indeed stop a bullet."

"Works for me," Lloyd agreed. "Let's check out the other belt."

Now that they had the general notion, that proved to be relatively quick: the white band enhanced the power of the wearer enormously. It was the opposite of the black band; instead of absorbing or deflecting threatening objects, it made the wearer a dangerous force.

"With this combination, a person could accomplish almost anything," Penn said. "No weapon could hurt him, and no barrier could stop him. I begin to see why these artifacts were hidden from early discovery."

"Why?" Lloyd asked.

Penn smiled. "Because they represent too much power for novices. There is evidently a course of learning associated with this house, and we, the learners, are protected from the things that could hurt us. Until we are ready for them."

"But these bands will help us, not hurt us."

"Unless one of us used them, without realizing their power. Suppose I wore the white band, and kicked the wall, or patted you on the head?"

Lloyd nodded. "Hole in the wall. Knockout."

"Precisely. Se we had better practice well with these, so as to make no unfortunate mistakes."

"Maybe by the time Kailash is well enough to join in, we'll have them down pat."

"Maybe not," Chandelle said, looking up from the page of

squiggles. "I think I have figured out another artifact."

"Another weapon?" Lloyd asked.

"Something better. I think there is an item that promotes rapid healing."

It was a simple little sphere, like a marble. But when Lloyd fetched it from the attic, it made his hand feel gently good. It had no controls; like the others, it simply worked on the person it touched.

They took it Kailash. "Take this," Lloyd told him, proffering the marble. "See if it helps you."

"What is it?" Llynn asked.

"Just take it."

Kailash accepted the little sphere. "This feels good."

"It's a healer. See if it works on your cut."

The man brought the marble to the bandage on his side. He smiled. "I feel it mending."

"Grandma figured it out. Maybe it can heal you fast."

Kailash put his free hand to the bandage and began drawing it off. He moved the sphere in closer to the wound. "The closer it gets, the better it gets," he said, amazed.

Indeed, the cut was fading as the sphere touched it. It looked much better than it had.

"It's mending inside, too," Kailash said. "I feel the flesh getting better."

"You know what that means," Lloyd said. "You'll be able to rescue your sister."

"Yes, I believe I will."

"So we'd better make plans." Lloyd tried to suppress the excitement he felt. The idea of going out into a foreign city and doing something significant, using the devices of the house—that thrilled him. Of course it would be Kailash who went, because it was his mission. If anyone went with him, it would be Llynn. Still, Lloyd was helping.

He had not yet figured out all the aspects of the white band, so he took it out back and experimented, with Penn's advice. He discovered that if he threw something, it could go with superhuman force. If he jumped, he could leap far higher than any normal person. So he had to don the black band too, so as not to hurt himself by falling from a height. Then, in stages, he tried for height—and found that he really could leap a building in a bound. When he ran, he could gain as much speed as the traction of his shoes allowed. He was a superman.

"Better practice your stops, too," Penn advised.

He did. Here the black band really helped, because sometimes he sent himself tumbling.

Llynn came out, and they showed her how the bands worked. Soon she was running and leaping too, exhilarated. "I'm Wonder Woman!" she cried.

They held a council of war. Lloyd demonstrated the black and white bands for Chandelle and Kailash, and they reviewed the hearing aid, translator, and lie detector. "You will have to do it, Kailash," Penn said. "But I'm not sure you should go alone."

"I will go alone if I have to," Kailash said. "But I would much prefer to have assistance. There may be unanticipated problems."

"Yes, of course. But which of us would best be able to help you?"

"Lloyd, I think."

Lloyd jumped. "Me?"

"I understand that women do not go adventuring in Arabia," Kailash said. "Especially not to a place such as we may visit. I am also not sure that your grandfather would care to go there."

"Delicately put," Penn agreed. "Lloyd it is." He turned to Lloyd. "Unless you prefer not."

"No! I'd love it," Lloyd said quickly. "It's real adventure." He was amazed, and gratified.

Kailash was completely better within two hours; the sphere had done the job. He had, however, an enormous hunger. "It's not magic," Chandelle said, serving him a big meal. "Healing uses energy, and you have used a lot. So you have to eat, to restore it."

"I like your grandmother," Kailash murmured to Lloyd as he ate ravenously.

They found the setting for Riyadh and parked the house there. This was some distance from the address they wanted, but with the white bands they would be able to handle the distance on foot. The city was modern and spacious and surprisingly clean; Lloyd had had no idea that such civilization extended into this supposed hinterland.

"Lot of oil money comes here," Penn explained. "They haven't wasted it. They have transformed this section of the desert."

Lloyd got on the Internet and moved Louie's date up to tonight, local time. There was no problem; evidently they were used to changes in this business.

Kailash went out back with Lloyd and practiced with the bands. "But can I touch people?" he asked. "To shake hands, and such?"

"Dunno." Lloyd hadn't thought of that. So they tried shaking hands. There was no problem, as long as they kept it gentle. The bands, when worn under their shirts, gave no obvious evidence of their presence. Only when something came at them, or when they exerted themselves, did the powers manifest. These were very refined devices.

"And Shree—can I carry her?"

"We can take extra bands for her," Lloyd said.

"But we may have no time for instruction or practice."

It was true. So Kailash tried it with Llynn. He picked her up. "She's like a feather," he said, smiling. "No substance at all."

"Thanks, lout," Llynn said wryly.

"No, I mean you are very easy to carry," he said. "Try it, Lloyd." He handed Llynn to Lloyd, using just one hand circling her waist.

It was true. The band amplified his strength, so that his cousin felt impossibly light. "She's like a dummy filled with air," he said, lifting her up overhead by one hand on her bottom.

"Double thanks to you, squirt!" she retorted with enormous disgust. "Now put me down."

"Sorry." He set her carefully back on her feet. "But this is really something."

"One more thing we must know," Kailash said. "Can we move each other? In case one becomes incapacitated, or there is some other problem."

They tried it, and found that they could not hit each other, but could move each other, slowly. Lloyd could carry Kailash, but could not throw him. The two bands complemented each other, never colliding, but compromising at the boundaries. This was extraordinarily well tuned technology.

Night came. They set up with all the devices, and made ready to go. "Be careful, Kailash," Llynn said, stepping into him and aiming a kiss for his face. But she bounced back without scoring; she had moved too quickly. Lloyd stifled a bark of laughter.

"Perhaps I can do it," Kailash said, "if it is all right." He embraced her carefully and kissed her extremely lightly on the lips. Lloyd knew why: a heavy kiss could smash her face. They did have to be careful, when outfitted.

Then they left. "We will listen for you," Penn said. "Lynn will wait outside the door, so you can talk to her if you need to."

"Thank you," Kailash said.

They looked around. The street was clear. They started running, carefully, so as to move swiftly without wasting energy or attracting attention. Kailash was in a formal suit, for he would have to pose as Louie. Lloyd was in messenger boy clothing, so that with luck no one would notice him.

In scant moments they were at an intersection. They slowed, looked, then crossed, and resumed their run. The streets were lighted, and that helped them, but also meant that anyone could see them. But they were able to get most of the way there before traffic became thick enough to force them to become ordinary walking pedestrians.

When they reached the section of town they were looking for, there were too many vehicles and people to avoid. This was where they had to part. Kailash would go in the front way, presenting Louie's credit card-getting that had been a neat trick—and going to the room. He would speak directions for Lloyd to hear, and Lloyd would get in the back way, out of sight if possible. This was the tricky part; if they messed up, or had bad luck, it could be very bad for Shree.

Lloyd slunk into an alley and followed Kailash by ear. "I am approaching the building," the man murmured, and Lloyd heard him clearly, thanks to the hearing aid. "I am mounting the steps."

Lloyd found the building, and checked the back. There was a fire escape door, but it would not open from the outside, so he waited. He saw that all the windows were barred. He had a notion what that meant: no girls escaped that way. He heard Kailash identify himself, and pay the agreed fee, plus some for a suitable bribe. Then he was escorted to the chamber. It was on the third floor. Too bad; Lloyd would have to risk the fire escape route.

He took hold of the knob and pulled. The door did not give. He pulled harder, and the latch broke, allowing the door to open. He paused; would there be an alarm? No. Good. He entered, and walked quietly up the stairs to the third floor.

"Room 304," Kailash murmured. "Now entering. Escort departing."

The fire stairs opened only onto the main hall. He would have to risk it. He peered through the glass, and saw that there was a cart with sheets and blankets, evidently waiting for a hotel maid, and a guard.

A guard. How was he to get by that man, without raising a ruckus?

The maid emerged from a room she was evidently working on. She was a rather pretty creature; probably one of their girls doing menial work during her off hours.

The guard approached her. The girl looked scared. Probably

she didn't dare tell him no.

The guard pushed her back into the room for a smooch. He was facing away for the moment.

Lloyd opened the fire door and zipped down the hall, getting quickly out of the line of sight. Then he straightened up, and walked quickly down to the room.

The door opened as he got there. Kailash was standing just inside, in a small antechamber; he had not gone farther yet. "I am afraid of what I will see," he said. "In my village, this sort of thing is very bad."

"I'll check," Lloyd said thoughtlessly. He walked on into the main apartment.

There stood a stunningly lovely young woman in a harem outfit. Lloyd had seen more actual flesh in pictures, but this was real, and it amazed him. Then he realized that she must think he was Louie. "I—uh, I'm not him," he faltered, halfway tongue tied. That wasn't exactly right, but what he meant was that he wasn't the john. Then he realized that she couldn't understand him, as she did not have a translator. "I—Kailash's here to rescue you."

"Kailash!" she exclaimed, understanding that much.

Kailash stepped out. "Shree."

Her jaw dropped. Then she flung herself at him, bursting into tears.

"We must go," Kailash said. "This is Lloyd. He will lead you out while I distract them. Go with him."

She understood him, because he was speaking in their own language. "But there are guards! It's not possible."

"I will see to the guard," Kailash said. He turned and left the room.

Shree flung on a robe. It could not prevent her from being beautiful. They hunched together by the door, peering out. Lloyd had to force his attention to business, lest he be totally distracted by her magnetic nearness. She even smelled good.

They saw Kailash approaching the guard. The two talked for a moment.

But whatever Kailash said, the guard wasn't having it. He drew a pistol. Kailash struck at his hand, but the gun went off. Shree screamed.

Doors opened all along the hall. In a moment it would be thronged with people. They would never get out that way. Lloyd realized that they should have worked out an alternate plan in case the first fouled up, as it was bound to do at some point. Now they were in for it.

Lloyd cast wildly around. He saw the barred window. "This way!" he said, crossing to it.

She seemed to understand him. "But—"

He opened the double windows inward, exposing the bars. He grasped a bar with one hand and pushed, hard. The entire grate ripped out of the wall. He dropped it to the ground. "This way," he said. "I'll carry you."

"What?" She was staring at the open window, having no idea what was happening.

"It's all right. We have to get out of here. Come."

When she still hesitated, understandably, Lloyd finally got smart. He dug in his pocket and brought out the spare translator he had brought. "Put this on."

She looked at him blankly. So he approached her, slowly, and put the little unit to her left ear. "Now you can understand me," he said.

Her pretty mouth dropped open. "I understand you," she repeated.

"Right. It's a translator. Put it on, and we'll get out of here."

She brought up her left hand, touching his hand at her ear, and took the unit. Her hand was like roses and silk, all sweet and soft. She set the unit, then looked at him again. Her eyes were like those of angels, large and dark. "Out?"

"I'll carry you," he repeated.

She hesitated. He walked back, put one arm around her shoulders and the other behind her knees, and picked her up. She offered no resistance. She was feather light, just as Llynn had been, with his band strength. He strode toward the window. He put one foot on the sill. He stepped up on it.

Shree screamed.

Lloyd leaped out of the window. Shree screamed again, clinging to him.

He concentrated on his feet, making sure of his landing in the dimly lighted alley. He wouldn't be hurt if he landed wrong, but Shree might be. He had to touch with spring in his legs, so as to cushion her landing too.

He got it. He let her descend a foot, then lifted her back up, as though she had bounced on rubber. Immediately he ran for the house, knowing the direction.

"My brother!" Shree exclaimed. Lloyd was suddenly conscious of her exquisitely soft flesh against him.

"Oh, yeah," he agreed after a moment, still running. He tuned in on Kailash, but all he heard was a confused babble. So he hoped Kailash was listening. "Kailash," he said. "We're clear. Get out of there!"

He got an answer. "Clear? How?"

"Out the window."

"Oh. Of course. I will follow." There was the sound of scuffling, and of a body hitting a wall. Kailash was getting clear of the guards. Then, after the sound of running feet, more news: "I am down. We will meet at the house."

"Right," Lloyd said. Then, to Shree: "Kailash is all right. He'll meet us soon."

She studied him in the light of the street as they came onto it. Her amazement was alleviating; she was beginning to accept the situation, weird as it was. "You seem so young, yet—"

"It's special technology. We'll show you, when we get there. It fixes it so I can talk to you, and carry you, and stuff. So we could rescue you."

"I think I am dreaming," she murmured.

Lloyd didn't worry who might be seeing them; he just wanted to get to the house as soon as possible. Only then would Shree be safe. So he didn't argue; he just ran on. It was easy, but the activity was getting him winded; he was after all expending some energy, and he was not a natural runner.

He thought to tune in Llynn. "Llynn! Are you there?"

"It's about time you answered me," Llynn responded. "I've been listening to you all along. You've got a sweet armful, right?"

Oh, yes! "Sorry. We're getting there."

"There's no pursuit. I think they don't know you're on foot."

He found the street, and then the house. There was Llynn. He slowed, then set Shree down near the walk. "That's my cousin. She's okay. Kailash'll come, and we'll be safe."

She seemed uncertain, but followed him up to the house. "Hello, Shree," Llynn said. Sure enough, Shree was shorter than Llynn, but better shaped. "Come in."

Then there was a blur, and Kailash arrived. Shree gave a gasp of relief, and went to him. "It's all right," Kailash said. "These are my friends. We must enter the residence."

They all went into the house. Penn reset the door, and Riyadh vanished. Then Kailash tried to explain things to his sister.

Lloyd was silent. Just looking at her was enough. Even somewhat disheveled, and bundled in her robe over her costume, she was beautiful. And he had touched her, held her, carried her. Would there ever be another experience like that? He doubted it.

There were quick introductions to the grandparents and Obsidian in the living room. Shree obviously wasn't really taking it in, except that she was safe. She clung to Kailash, and sobbed.

Then she collected herself. "I thank you, all of you, for rescuing me. Now may I have a private place, and a knife?"

Kailash looked stricken. "No, Shree!"

"It must be," she said calmly. "I can not go home."

He nodded. "I had hoped it would not come to that."

"It did. May I have a knife?"

Penn and Chandelle looked grim, but did not move or speak. They evidently understood something Lloyd didn't. That bugged him.

"We have knives in the kitchen," Lloyd said. "What for?"

Kailash looked at him. "My sister wishes to kill herself."

"What? This is a joke, right?" But no one was laughing. "Why?"

"She is unclean. She can not go home. But now that she is free, she can escape the horror, and I will not tell our family, so as to preserve her honor there."

"Her honor! What are you talking about?"

Kailash looked at Shree. She turned away. "They made her do unconscionable things. She is unclean. No man will marry her. No one will speak to her. She must end her pain."

"Because of the—" Lloyd said, horrified by the enormity of it.

Llynn spoke. "In some cultures I read about, when a woman gets raped, she is rendered outcast. They think it's her fault."

"Her fault!" he exploded. "It's not!"

"She has nothing to return to," Kailash said. "The people of our village would look upon her with loathing. No man will touch her."

"This is crazy! *I'd* touch her." Then, realizing what he was saying, he got flustered. "I mean, if I was old enough. If she wanted me to. She's beautiful."

Shree turned. "Would you? Knowing what I have done?"

"Sure I would! Who cares what they made you do? You couldn't help it. And even if you could, what's so wrong about it? You're gorgeous."

She looked at her brother. "He is sincere," Kailash said.

Something odd touched her face. "Can it be? He would kiss me?"

"Sure I would!"

"Test him," Kailash said. "He is from another culture."

Shree focused again on Lloyd. Then she crossed the room to him, moving like a summer mist. She stood before him, angled her face, and kissed him on the mouth, touching him nowhere else.

The universe whirled and faded away. Lloyd floated into nirvana.

Chapter 9
Triad

Chandelle tried to move, but couldn't get going fast enough. It was Penn who got there and caught Lloyd as he sagged to the floor.

"I have killed him!" Shree cried, horrified. "My polluted caress—"

"No you haven't," Llynn said. "You have merely put him in heaven for a while."

"But I am unclean, and I touched him. I despoiled him."

Chandelle stepped in. "This is woman's work," she said to Penn. "You boys go about your business. Come, Llynn. Come, Shree."

They walked the young woman to the kitchen, and sat her at the table with them. Then Chandelle spoke directly to Shree. "Lloyd will be all right. He's young, and I think never been kissed by a lovely woman. He will have a crush on you. That can't be helped. But you have not harmed him."

"I should not have—"

"We're Americans," Chandelle said firmly. "We have different beliefs. When a woman is raped, we believe we should punish the man who did it, not the woman. If you can't return to your own culture, you can remain in ours. We don't view you as unclean, merely unfortunate."

Shree shook her head. "It is not so easy."

Surely not. "Yet it is not easy for us to facilitate your suicide, for something we don't believe is your fault."

"It *is* my fault. I was weak, and now I must die. It is the only way."

For the moment Chandelle was at a loss. She knew she could not change a deeply set cultural belief with a few words, but the idea of allowing this lovely young woman to die appalled her.

"I don't see why you have to kill yourself, when you know it wasn't anything you wanted," Llynn said. "Can't you see the nonsense of that?"

Shree looked at her. "You are Lloyd's sister?"

"His cousin. We have the same grandparents, Penn and Chandelle."

"You love him?"

Llynn hesitated. "We're not that close. But I wouldn't try to hurt him."

"If he wanted to die, would you let him?"

"No!"

"My brother loves me. Therefore he will let me do what I must do."

"But he wanted so much to save you. He risked his own life, and almost lost it, looking for you."

Shree nodded. "I would not have him do that, when I am already lost. Yet he understands." She pondered a moment. "If your cousin wanted to be with me, would you let him?"

"Sure, if you wanted to do something together. Why not?"

"I think that's not exactly what she means," Chandelle said. Kailash was an intelligent, perceptive young man; similar qualities were becoming evident in this young woman.

"Well, what does she mean?" Llynn asked.

"To use me, as a man uses a woman."

That made Llynn pause. She glanced at Chandelle, but Chandelle held her expression neutral. She remembered how the grandchildren had watched the porno show, and been embarrassed when joined by the elders. Which of course had been the intention: to steer them clear without being dictatorial. There was learning to be had, and self discipline to establish, and meanwhile this allowed more time to figure out how to handle Shree's urge for death.

"That—would not be according to our culture," Llynn said af-er a moment. "Children aren't supposed to—to do adult things."

"Even when they are able to feel adult urges?"

"Well, they may feel them, but they could get in a lot of trouble for them. They need to—to learn how to handle them."

"So you would not let your cousin be with me, if I invited him?"

Llynn looked somewhat wildly around, as if seeking help from something in the kitchen. But there was none. This time she avoided Chandelle's eyes, which Chandelle found interesting. "I—guess I would let him. It's his business."

Shree looked at Chandelle. "Would you?"

"No."

"Why?"

"Because he's too young."

"Not because I am unclean?"

Now Chandelle saw the point of this. The woman was looking for a parallel to their culture that would justify her wish to kill herself. "No."

"Even though he is old enough, by my culture?"

Oops. She had fallen into it after all. "I suppose, if he were of your culture, it would be all right. But he is not, so he must be guided by his own culture."

Shree nodded. "As I must be guided by mine."

"Now, wait," Llynn said. "I'm of his culture, and I said I would let him."

"And would he let you be with my brother?"

Llynn blushed. Shree had scored again. But she had to answer. "Yes, he would. We're young. We don't see necessarily things the way the older folk do."

"So it is after all a different culture, and you are true to yours."

"Yes."

Shree considered. "If I made a meal of boiled roaches, would you eat it?"

"No way!"

"Even though a member of my culture would?"

Chandelle, listening, wondered: did they really boil roaches in the Himalayas, or was Shree bluffing?

Llynn shuddered. "I couldn't stand it."

"So you are unable to violate the dictates of your culture, however irrelevant they may appear to those of another culture."

Llynn raised her hands in surrender. "You're right. You have the right to do what you must. But I sure as hell won't help you."

"Neither will I," Chandelle said.

"Yet if you turn your backs, you know what I will do."

Llynn looked desperately at Chandelle. "Isn't there anything we can say?"

Chandelle tried. "If you do this—this thing—surely you know that you will be bringing grief to those who rescued you from your situation. Do you feel it is right to respond to our good will with your death?"

"I do not like this. But do you not see that by rescuing me, you have enabled me to escape my unbearable shame? You have helped me, and I think you for it, and I would do you some return favor if I could."

A return favor. There, perhaps, was an avenue. "We might have such a favor to ask. But first, you must explain to us exactly what happened to you, that makes you so determined to die. Even in your culture, there must be some mitigating circumstances."

"I do owe you that information," Shree said. "Though I would prefer to tell it to no one."

"We can keep a secret, if you wish," Llynn said.

"I do so wish."

"Tell us your story," Chandelle said. "How you got into this trap."

Shree paused, evidently nerving herself, then told her story. She had sought good employment in the big city, so as to be able to help her family survive the lean times. But the office in Delhi had turned out to be recruiting for work in a foreign city, Moscow. The pay, however, was significantly better than the ad had indicated, and she turned out to be well qualified. The woman urged her to go to Moscow with her application; the agency would even arrange transportation there, by air. "But I don't speak Russian," she protested. "It doesn't matter; they need secretaries in many languages. Good ones in particular languages are hard to find, and are paid very well." This was simply too good an opportunity to miss, so she agreed, and was immediately conducted to a commercial flight. "But I must tell my family," she said. The woman promised that they would inform Shree's family.

But when she reached the office in Moscow, they told her through a translator that the job was not there, but in Arabia. However, she was indeed well qualified, and the Arabs paid very well. They arranged for her flight to Riyadh the same day; she didn't even have time to dispatch a telephone message to her home village for her family, to update them on this second development. But in Riyadh, she was assured, she would have ample time to relay her good news.

In Arabia she discovered that women had very few rights. She was taken into a soundproof room where a man speaking her language badly told her she was to act as hostess to visiting dignitaries. "Hostess?" she asked blankly. "You will entertain them and make them happy." "Entertain?" "You will see. Take off your clothes."

She became alarmed. "I think I do not want this job after all." She tried to leave the room, but it was locked. The man snapped his fingers, and two more men entered from a far door she hadn't seen before. They grabbed her arms and ripped her clothing from her body. She tried to resist, but they simply overpowered her. They forced her to get down on her hands and knees, naked, and they opened panels in the floor to reveal padded leather loops. They tightened these around her wrists and ankles. She was bound to the floor, unable to change position other than to flop uncomfortably forward on the carpet.

One man kneeled behind her and touched her bare bottom.

"This man wishes make love to you," the interviewer said. "Do you agree?"

"No!" Shree cried, flopping forward.

The other man leaned over and lifted her torso so that she was again on hands and knees. Then he brought a metal box, and taped wires from it to her wrists. "Prepare yourself," the interviewer said. "This will be painful."

The box buzzed. Electric current surged through her body from wrist to wrist. She stiffened in absolute agony, unable even to breathe. After a moment it stopped, and she collapsed, gasping for breath.

"This is the penalty for refusal," the interviewer said. "I ask you again: do you agree to let this man penetrate you?"

"No," she said. But the word was hardly out before the current flowed again, stiffening her in agony. She could not take much more of this.

The man kept asking, and the current kept returning, until finally she could no longer endure the pain. "Yes," she sobbed. She hated it, but realized that they would kill her in this dreadful manner if she did not mouth the words they demanded.

To her dull surprise, the man did not do it. Instead, the wires were removed, and the straps were loosened. She was helped up, and her battered clothing was returned. "I think this is sufficient for today," the interviewer said. "Tomorrow I shall question you again, and if you fail to say yes, you will be treated with the wires again. Then, when you agree, my friend will use you, for you will have forfeited our grace by reneging. Only when you obey without question will you be free of pain. Do you understand?"

Now she did understand. She would do whatever these people asked of her, or they would torture her. "Yes," she said brokenly. "But why?"

"Because you are beautiful, and there is a market. Perform well, and you will be well treated. You can have a good life here, and generous money will be sent to your home. But you *will* perform."

"And so it was," she concluded. "I performed well. I could not face the torture. And they were sending the money to my family. So you see, I was not raped; I agreed to do their bidding, and I gave my body to the men who came to me, with smiles. I betrayed my honor, and now I must die."

"But you were tortured!" Llynn protested.

"I was weak. To save myself from pain, I gave away my soul. I can not bear to see my face in the mirror; I must die."

Chandelle exchanged a glance with Llynn. Should they tell Shree that no money had come to her family? Even in this, the slavers had betrayed her. "I think perhaps if I had been treated as you were, I would feel much the same," Chandelle said. "But I would not seek to die."

"I would seek revenge," Llynn said grimly.

"Revenge can not recover my honor," Shree said. "Only death can salvage part of it."

And she would not be moved. Chandelle understood that now. But she tried a wild gamble. She was betting that this young woman was as honorable as she seemed, and would react in a certain way. "Give us some time to come to terms with this. Postpone your death a week, and—and I will let Lloyd come to you."

"Grandma!" Llynn cried, shocked.

"This is a matter of honor," Chandelle said. "We are asking her to sacrifice hers, for a time. We must sacrifice ours, for that time."

Shree stared at her. "But I am unclean."

"Lloyd doesn't care about that. We don't care. You can repay us for rescuing you by giving us more time, and making him happy. He can surely learn much from you."

Shree considered, her face frozen. Then she spoke. "Three days, and I will not let him come."

"Agreed," Chandelle said immediately, feeling weak in the

knees, for all that she was sitting. Her gamble had paid off: the woman had been impressed enough to yield some ground, and decent enough to avoid a price she knew would hurt the family. "And no one speaks of this, of her story or my offer, to anyone else," she said to Llynn. "Only that there is no present problem."

"Agreed," Llynn whispered, her face ashen. She had seen a side of her grandmother she had never suspected.

"Now we must arrange accommodations," Chandelle said briskly. "I think Shree must share your room, Llynn, and you may show her the things and ways of the house. Kailash will room with Lloyd."

"But Grandma," Llynn said. "What happens after three days?"

"Then Shree will do as she chooses, and we will not interfere. This is our bargain."

Shree nodded. "Thank you, Grandmother Chandelle."

"Now you are surely tired," Chandelle said. "Llynn will show you to her room."

The two young women got up and left the kitchen. Chandelle sat there for a time, letting her emotions ease slowly, like a pressure cooker letting off steam. She had done what she had to do, but this wasn't over, by a long shot. What was to be her next move?

And what about Lloyd? She felt guilty for bringing him into it. She had been casting about for something, anything, to jolt Shree out of the suicide mode, and grasped at a straw she shouldn't have. Lloyd had carried Shree back, and Shree had kissed Lloyd; she was grateful to him and he was smitten with her. She was a woman with nothing to lose, and he was a willful boy. If they decided to get together, neither parental—Grandparental—nor societal disapproval would stop them. So perhaps it was better to bring that into the open. Now she had Shree's commitment to stay clear of the boy, in that respect, and that was good. So maybe she hadn't done such awful wrong there; maybe she had gambled and won.

But the deathwish—all else would be nothing, if that could not be abated. She had three days to change it—if she could only figure out how.

She got up and went to the living room. The three males were seated there, evidently having a dialogue of their own. They all looked at her as she entered. "It's all right," she said.

None of them spoke. They knew better.

"We had a—a private discussion," she said, feeling awkward.

"How long?" Kailash asked.

She had to tell. "Three days."

All three relaxed visibly. They had known that Chandelle would try to persuade Shree not to die, but probably had not thought she would succeed.

"And then?" Lloyd asked. He looked as if he had been crying, which of course he would never admit. He was caught in the throes of sudden love, and if Shree died, he would be desolate. Obsidian, beside him, looked unhappy too.

"I can't say," she said.

"But thereafter, we can't interfere?" Penn asked.

She didn't answer. They had agreed not to talk about their compromise. Chandelle had not thought of what she would say to the others.

"She has not answered," Penn said to the others.

Kailash and Lloyd nodded. They had gotten the message. No interference.

"Llynn and Shree have retired to Llynn's room for the night," Chandelle said. "I suggest that Kailash move in with Lloyd."

"But I had not intended to stay," Kailash protested. "Only to rescue my sister."

"It's okay," Lloyd said. "There's another bed there."

"But it would be imposing."

Penn looked at him. "She's not rescued yet. Give it three days."

"Then what?" Lloyd asked. He looked drawn.

Kailash didn't answer.

But Penn pursued it. “Let’s say she changes her mind, and lives. Are you going to take her home?”

“She can’t go home,” Kailash said.

“We can set you down anywhere in the world,” Penn said. “But I don’t think we can let the translators go; they don’t belong to us. In any event, they would attract attention.”

“And even if you had the translators, the people would not understand you,” Lloyd said. “You would understand them, but that’s all. Unless you went to your own territory.”

“Anywhere in India, they would know,” Kailash said. “She would be a pariah.”

Penn bore down. “So you have three alternatives. One, she dies, and you go home and preserve her reputation. Two, she lives, and you struggle to find somewhere in the world where it is your language but not your culture. Three, you stay with us.”

“But you do not owe us this! We can not repay what you have already done. We can not impose further.”

“This is not imposition,” Penn said. “The house summons those it desires as residents. It summoned us. It summoned you. And I suspect it summoned Shree. She has no life elsewhere, if she lives, and you have no life elsewhere, if she lives. You are free only if she dies. Do you want that?”

“No. Yet what must be, must be.”

“I think it must be that the two of you are joining the four of us. To serve the purpose of the house. We can leave, if we want to. You can’t.”

“This is a very generous interpretation.”

“Maybe not entirely,” Chandelle said. “Llynn likes you. And Lloyd—”

“I do not wish to interfere with your cultural prerogatives,” Kailash said. “This is one reason it would be better for me to go.”

Penn gestured with his hands, signaling a certain mixture of emotions. “I think we do not object to Llynn’s feeling for you. She could do worse for a man, but is unlikely to do better.”

"But the culture—she could never accept mine."

"But could you accept hers?"

Kailash paused. "I think, if it were permitted, I could accept anything about her. But she is young, and—"

"In time she will be less young," Penn said. "If you remain here, you will see that time."

"This is an offer it would be difficult to refuse."

"What about Shree?" Lloyd asked sharply.

"She is eighteen," Chandelle said. "I think you know that she is unlikely to have any romantic interest in you."

"I know. But—"

"If she lives, I think she will be your friend. She does appreciate what you have done for her."

"Okay!" he said gladly.

"And it surely would not hurt if you tried to be the kind of person another person could like."

"Yeah. Llynn's teaching me to dance. I can learn more. I don't have to be a brat."

Chandelle turned to Kailash. "Perhaps you will be able to help us find a way to save your sister's life."

"She will not change," he said sadly.

"I'm thinking of the potentials of this house. It has enabled us to do things we never thought were possible. Maybe it has something that will help solve this problem."

"Tell me what to do," he said.

"For now, get some sleep. Tomorrow we will explore the rest of the attic."

That concluded the discussion. They retired to their rooms for the remainder of the night. Penn did not question her privately about her dialogue with Shree and Llynn, but perhaps he had guessed its nature.

In the morning, Chandelle was first up, as usual in this house, and was preparing a breakfast in the kitchen when Shree came down, accompanied by Obsidian. "I thought you would need more rest," Chandelle said, surprised.

"I have had quite enough physical rest," Shree said, adjusting the translator at her ear. "They wanted me to be beautiful. It was my spirit they despoiled."

"I understand. Your brother would have spared you that, had he been able. We all would have."

"I know. But it was too late. Why did you intercede for me?"

"I don't want anyone to die without reason," Chandelle said. Then quickly caught herself. "I realize that as you see it, you have reason. But for me—"

"I understand. Is that the whole of it?"

Chandelle paused. This was a perceptive girl. The kind the house wanted to recruit. "No. I know what you have gone through, in a manner."

"I wondered. You do not show it."

"It was a long time ago. I preferred to forget about it."

"Yet you remembered."

"There was a certain similarity that your situation evoked. I had gone to a party where alcohol was served. It was in the punch; I did not realize. I was encouraged to drink a lot of it, and I became—very free. When I realized what was happening, I tried to get away, but could not. Until several of the males had had their way with me. Then they threatened awful things if I ever told, and I was afraid, and never did tell. Except for Penn, before he married me. I never went to another such party."

"You did not kill yourself."

"I did consider it. But that isn't in my culture. So I buried it."

Shree shook her head. "I can not do that."

"I know."

"And the boy. You offered him to me."

Chandelle smiled ruefully. "I shouldn't have done that. I was just trying to find some way to move you."

"I will let him be."

"Just be his friend."

"What I contemplate is not a friendly thing. Better that he have no association with me, these three days."

"That is not possible, in this house."

"You wish to persuade me to live."

"Yes."

"I do not wish you to have an unrealistic hope."

Chandelle looked her in the eyes.

"Shree, if you could change your position on this, would you?"

She shrugged. "If you could persuade yourself to eat boiled roaches, would you?"

"Yes! I would do what I had to do. Because there are others affected by what I do. What you contemplate is selfish. When you die, you will be beyond suffering, but the rest of us will suffer. Especially Lloyd, and your brother."

Shree studied her thoughtfully. "Do you have an avenue for persuasion that is not of the nature the evil men employed?"

"Yes. Will you consider it?"

"For these three days, I will."

Chandelle went to a kitchen drawer and brought out the sheaf of squiggle papers. "The secrets of this house are here. I can read these better than the others can, but there are still things I don't understand. I hope there is something here for you. I don't know what. I just don't want to believe that this house could have brought you here, only to die. It must have something."

"Perhaps so." But she was merely being polite.

"The top sheet is the first of the devices we haven't yet figured out. See if you can comprehend the symbols."

Shree looked at the top sheet of squiggles. "These mean nothing to me."

Chandelle had a sudden, wild notion. "Take off the translator. Look at them with your natural eye."

Shree removed the translator and set it on the table. She looked again at the paper. After a moment she looked up. "Yes, now I can read it. This describes a trainer, greatly facilitating learning."

"You can read it!" Chandelle exclaimed. "Just like that!"

Shree looked blankly at her.

"Oh, of course. You don't understand me, without your translator. But I understand you. Keep reading."

Shree lifted the translator to her ear.

"Keep reading!" Chandelle repeated.

"Yes," Shree agreed, setting down the device. She looked at the next page. "This describes a persuader. With it, a person can influence others to do what he wishes."

"That could be useful, on occasion," Chandelle said. "But we prefer that others see the reason in our wishes, rather than being blindly influenced." She realized that Shree could not understand her now, but it was easier to express herself anyway. This was wonderful; the girl could read with much greater facility than Chandelle could. With her help they might unriddle the remaining secrets of the house in short order.

Shree looked at a third page. "This describes a reconciler. With it, the wearer becomes reconciled to what must be, even if he thought it impossible before."

She looked up, meeting Chandelle's gaze. "You wish me to become reconciled to life."

Chandelle nodded.

Shree returned the translator to her ear. "I do not believe this can be effective. But I will try it. Let us find this device."

They followed the dog to the attic, which Shree had not seen before. Chandelle explained the mechanism of the stairway, and the girl was suitably impressed. In the attic Shree removed her translator again, and quickly oriented on the device they sought. It was a green headband, stretchable and quite unprepossessing. She put it on. "I will live."

"What?"

Shree was not wearing the translator, but Chandelle's surprise was clear enough. "I can now accept what my reason indicates should be accepted. If I am to join your group, in this house, I must put aside my former culture and live. This I shall do."

"Just like that? No time for consideration?"

Shree removed the band and donned the translator. "I think you should try this," she said.

Fair enough. Chandelle put on the band.

A new universe opened out to her. It was as if she had a new consciousness, above the other parts of her mind. She looked on all things rationally, without emotion. She could do anything she deemed necessary. If it seemed appropriate to kill a person, she could do that. She would have no problem with boiled roaches.

She removed the band—and then was appalled. "That's an alien mind!" she said. "No emotions, just practical considerations."

Shree nodded. "I will wear it, if you wish me to. But should I remove it, I will seek again to die."

"But if you wear this, you will not be yourself! You might as well be a living robot."

"Perhaps after a time I will no longer need it. Its logic is convincing."

Chandelle set the band on her head again. "Yes, wear it," she said. She removed it and handed it over.

Shree took it and put it on. "The others well not readily accept this," she said.

"I'm not at all sure I like it myself. When I put it on, it makes sense, but when I take it off, my natural instincts return."

"That is why it is effective. It suppresses nature."

They descended the stairs, returning to the house proper. The others were now up and around, curious about what was going on.

"We discovered three tools," Shree informed them. "I am wearing one, and I will remain with you while I wear it, as it makes me utterly rational. I will not be demonstrating emotion or other human foibles, however."

The menfolk exchanged a glance. "What are the other two

tools?" Penn asked.

"One enables the user to persuade others of things, even against their preferences. The other enables people to learn and train effectively, especially when the necessary discipline is complicated."

"These are dangerous tools," Kailash said. "They could cause much mischief if misused."

"Of course. Is it our purpose to misuse them?"

Kailash looked at her. "You are different. Your mind is not the one I have known."

She removed the green band and proffered it to him. "I recommend that you try it."

He put it on. "This brings unprecedented clarity of thought," he said. He took it off and gave it to Penn.

Penn hesitated, then tried it. "This is remarkable. I have never had a clearer perspective." He removed it and gave it to Lloyd.

Lloyd was evidently good and curious by this time. He donned the band. "This must be adult life," he said. "I have no juvenile emotions, only clarity of thought." He removed it and gave it to Llynn.

Llynn held the band. Then she handed it back to Shree without trying it. "I'll stick with my own mind, thank you," she said.

"Perhaps that is just as well," Chandelle said. "We are not machines."

Shree put it on. "If I return to my own mind, I will die. But I see now that this is not advisable at this time. We do not yet know the purpose of this house, and we should learn it before any of us do anything that is not reversible."

Penn shrugged. "I'm beginning to wonder whether this is a bargain with the devil."

Chandelle has a similar misgiving. They had found an answer to the problem of Shree's deathwish, but was this the best answer? She wished she could be sure, one way or the other.

Chapter 10
Fine Tuning

Penn was both gratified and concerned by recent developments. They had saved Shree, who seemed like a fine girl, but at the price of nullifying her emotions. For now it would have to do, but he hoped there was a better way.

Meanwhile, he had another concern. Two days ago they had escaped disaster by dumping two Russian men into the back forest. He had no sympathy for the men's employment, as they were merely thugs enforcing white slavery (for all that skin color hardly mattered: the girls were innocent captives whatever their origins), but he did not like to think of killing them, and that was what the effect would be. They would have to fetch the men out and return them to Moscow. Thereafter, it wouldn't matter.

He broached the matter to Chandelle. "Those two men—"

"Yes, of course," she agreed. "We can't leave them there."

"With the shield and amplifier, I believe we can handle them. All we need to do is take them from the back to the front, in Moscow."

"Don't do it alone," she said.

"Kailash and Lloyd can help."

She nodded, and he went to find the others. They were in the living room, nominally watching TV, but Llynn's eyes seemed to be more on Kailash, and Lloyd's on Shree. Well, that situation should work itself out in time. Though what would happen when the month was over, he hesitated to conjecture.

"I think it is time to return those two lost thugs to Moscow," he announced. "I realize that you may not be amicably disposed toward them, Kailash—"

"I do not know them. I do not wish to harm them, only to be

safe from them."

"Then you may help me move them from the back yard to the front door. I think each of us can simply pick one up and carry him."

"Agreed."

"I can do it," Lloyd said.

"I think I need you to manage the doors," Penn said diplomatically. Lloyd could indeed do it, but two carriers were enough. "We'll need the forest in back, and the city of Moscow in front. Wear the bands; if anything goes wrong, you will need to be ready to step in."

"Got it," Lloyd said, satisfied.

"Maybe the rest of us should put on bands, too," Llynn said. "Shree can use the practice, and if any man tries to maul us, we'll be ready."

"Yes." Penn was trying to act as if this transfer were routine, but it made him nervous. He wanted to be safely done with it.

They donned their bands, and took their positions. "I'll do the front door," Llynn told Lloyd. "So you don't have to run around them to get there, after they come through the back door."

The boy considered, ready to protest. "I will assist you at the back," Shree said. The protest faded without trace.

They lined up. Lloyd stood at the door. When Penn signaled, he punched the number, and the forest appeared beyond.

Penn opened the door and they stepped cautiously out. There was no person in sight. The thugs must have gotten lost.

"Where are they?" Kailash asked, looking around. He had not seen this setting before, though Penn had described it and warned him about its special effects.

"They must have been astonished when the house vanished," Penn said, piecing it out. "And fled into the forest, looking for a way out of it."

Kailash turned and looked at the boulder. Then he looked again an the surrounding forest. "That seems reasonable. But this re-

;ion seems large. How can we find them?"

"With the hearing aid," Penn said. He knocked on the invis-ble door behind them. It opened in a moment, and Lloyd was ·evealed, Shree behind him, with Obsidian. "We need hearing ıids," Penn said. "We'll have to go after them."

"Got it." The boy ran back out of sight.

Shree smiled at them. "Do be careful."

"You're not wearing the reconciler," Penn said.

"I find I do not have to wear it continuously," she said, lifting ıer hand to show that she was holding the headband. "I prefer o feel emotions, when they are positive. The dog is also a com-'ort." She petted Obsidian.

"Perhaps we should also carry water," Kailash suggested as hey waited.

"Good thought. They'll be thirsty."

Shree went into the kitchen, returning in a moment with two :anteens. "Chandelle anticipated that." She handed them over.

Lloyd returned with two hearing aids. "Grandma says to be :areful."

"I already informed them of that," Shree said, smiling at him.

Lloyd visibly melted. "Yeah."

Penn and Kailash took the headbands and put them on. Then hey turned to the forest, and listened.

Immediately Penn heard hard breathing. He pointed the di-·ection, and Kailash nodded agreement. They started off, mov-ng with amazing ease. This was the first time Penn had used :he amplifier to travel outside, and he liked it.

"I believe my sister likes Lloyd," Kailash said.

"Maybe she likes being liked. Especially at this time."

"Surely so. He is too young to be artificial, and she appreciates that. His sincerity persuades her that she is not necessarily worth-less."

"So she is able to take off the reconciler for a while," Penn agreed. "I do prefer her without it."

Their power stops soon brought them to the two thugs. They were lying against the trunk of a huge tree, looking bedraggled. They scrambled up when they saw Penn and Kailash, bringing out their knives.

Penn proffered his canteen to the nearest thug. The man stared at it, then put away his knife and took it. He unscrewed the cap and tilted it up, gulping the water.

Kailash offered his canteen to the other man. The reaction was similar. Thirst was a great persuader, after two days in the endless daytime of the impervious wilderness.

"Follow us," Penn said, gesturing. He knew they wouldn't understand his words, but would take his meaning. They had already discovered that they could not eat or drink anything in the forest, or have any effect on it; they were desperate to get out of it.

Penn and Kailash walked back toward the house, slowly. The two men followed. They did not try to attack, surely impressed by the confidence of their rescuers. They didn't know that they couldn't hurt Penn and Kailash; maybe they thought that if they killed these two, they would be forever stranded here. They probably understood that the situation had changed, and their prior mission was moot.

Penn reached the boulder, and knocked. The door opened. "Follow me," he said, gesturing again, and walked through. Kailash stayed back, to finish the procession.

Penn marched straight through the house, and the two thugs followed in single file. Llynn opened the front door on Moscow. Penn stepped out, then stood beside the walk. The men emerged, spied halfway familiar terrain, and lumbered down the walk to the street. Kailash came to stand beside Penn.

The men turned back to the house. Then they set down the empty canteens, waved, and walked down the street.

"That was easier than I expected," Penn said.

"For me, too," Kailash agreed. "Vengeance was not necessary."

"They have been punished enough," Penn said. "I suspect they will seek other employment, after this."

"If they tell their story, they will be regarded as lunatics," Kailash said. "I am not entirely certain that I am sane myself, considering what I have recently encountered."

"This house is a considerable experience for all of us." But Penn realized that he liked it. His life had become somewhat dull. That was no longer the case.

They went down to fetch the canteens, and returned to the house. Llynn closed the front door behind them and reset the number. Moscow was done.

"The forest," Kailash said. "Is it truly infinite?"

"As far as we can tell," Penn said. "Llynn and I tried to explore it, and couldn't find the end. We think it's 30,000 years ago, in Pennsylvania."

Kailash frowned. "Was there not an ice age then?"

"The ice age!" Penn exclaimed. "The glaciers would not have been far away. How could such a well developed forest be there?"

Shree went to a living room shelf. "There is an atlas," she said, taking down a large book.

It was more than an atlas. It was a geological atlas, showing the lands of Earth back for millions of years. They gathered around it, poring over its marvelous maps. They saw the progression of the continents, forming into one or two monstrous masses, then fragmenting into the present configuration. They saw the coming of the ice ages. "You're right," Penn said. "It couldn't be Pennsylvania. Not then."

"Where *is* this house, really?" Llynn asked. "I mean, it can be in Philadelphia, or Okinawa, or Moscow, or anywhere. Is it just shuttling around, with no fixed address, or is it just the doors that change?"

Penn sat down. "I hadn't thought about that. I assumed the house itself was moving from site to site, but if that's true, what about the back door, which doesn't seem to move spatially?

Where *is* the house?"

"It does seem easier for the doors to move, than the whole house," Llynn said. "So the house could be parked on one place, where the back door is, and the front door is—is—"

"A matter transmitter," Lloyd said.

"I agree," Penn said. "It would have to be a matter transmitter for the whole house, people included, if it all moved. Much easier to handle just the people who pass through the door. Less energy expenditure."

"And the permanent site would have to be well protected," Lloyd said. "So the locals wouldn't get in and mess it up."

"We're the locals," Llynn said. "So who made this house? We don't have the technology."

There was a brief silence. "Maybe the worms," Penn said at last.

"I don't think so," Kailash said. "There are too many things of human manufacture. There must be contact with the human realm."

"Even the newspapers," Llynn agreed. "Someone must have subscribed to them."

The more they discussed it, the more it seemed that there had to be more to the house than they had discovered. "An empty house could not have stocked itself with human commercial food, clothing, bicycles, car, television, computer, and all the related services," Penn said. "Also, it could not have zeroed in on our personal tastes."

"And summoned us," Kailash said. "There is a presence. A motive. A need."

"As though the house is alive and conscious," Chandelle said. "It is a mother mouse."

That made Penn nervous. "Or a very well programmed machine."

"Yet some one or some thing must have constructed it," Shree said, donning her headband for completely rational consideration. "That care evidently continues, as evidenced by the changing numbers on the plaque."

"So that consciousness must have a source," Kailash said. "Somewhere within the house."

"Gotta be something we can find," Lloyd said. "Maybe we just gotta look."

"Let's form teams and check every part," Llynn said. "Until we find it. I'll go with Kailash."

But Kailash demurred. "Were I to be with you, I would be looking at you rather than the house," he said. "Then we would not succeed."

Llynn blushed, but could not deny his logic, though she surely suspected that he had exaggerated the case. She was the one who was distracted by him, rather than the other way around. So the teams were formed by random selection: Llynn and Chandelle, Kailash and Lloyd, and Penn and Shree. While Obsidian had free choice.

Llynn and Chandelle took the upstairs, to see whether there were any more offshoots like that attic. Lloyd and Kailash took the downstairs, including the garage, to see whether there were any more items of special equipment. And Penn and Shree took the cellar, which had not really been explored in detail.

The stairs led down to the furnace chamber. "Do you know," Penn said thoughtfully, "I've never been aware of this house heating or cooling. It's always just right. Maybe this isn't a furnace."

"That concept makes me nervous," she said.

He looked at her. She was wearing one of the outfits in Llynn's room, a black blouse and gray skirt with black shoes. She had evidently done some sewing, to let out the clothing to fit her fuller figure, but it remained a trifle tight across the chest and hips. The reconciler band in her hand was gray, matching the skirt. She was an extremely attractive young woman. "Perhaps you should don the band, then," he suggested.

She did so. "Nervousness is foolish, when there is no apparent threat," she said. "Nevertheless, this unit should be treated with caution." She eyed the furnace.

"We can check it readily enough. There should be a compartment for burning fuel, of whatever kind."

There was a small door in the front. Penn opened it and peered in. There was no chamber as such; instead there was a square tube leading into darkness.

"This does not appear to be ordinary apparatus," Shree said.

"I wonder where the tunnel goes?"

"There is a straightforward way to find out." She bent forward and started to put her head into the hole.

"Shree!" he protested. "Don't!"

"It should be safe," she said, and stretched her arms forward in the manner of a diver, entering the hole.

"No!" He grabbed her about the waist and hauled her back. But she was already moving forward with surprising agility. He had to shift his grip and brace himself to get her out.

They wound up standing face to face, his arms wrapped around her, holding her close. Her brown eyes were staring into his. Then he became aware again of just how feminine she was, all lovely softness and allure.

Embarrassed, he let her go. "Sorry. I just couldn't let you take that chance."

"I understand. You are not the type of man to take advantage, even when the woman has nothing left to lose. You suffered an emotional reaction, fear for my security. I know that, as I wear the band." She touched her head. "But by the same token, I am sure that this house does not seek to harm its occupants. So if there is a passage suitable in size to accommodate one of us, it must be safe to use it. The sensible thing is to explore it."

She was, of course, being rational. But still it bothered him. "Then I should be the one to risk it."

"No. You are important to this house and your family. I am of little such worth, and my life may in any event be brief. Therefore I should take any risks that may occur."

"That's ridiculous!"

She touched the band. "Perhaps you should borrow this for a moment."

He had to yield, for he know what the band would tell him. He was guilty of foolish gallantry, especially because she was so lovely. "I apologize. You are right."

"Thank you." She turned and climbed back into the hole. He couldn't help seeing her thighs and underwear as she brought her legs inside. Ah, to be forty years younger, and single! She couldn't go on all fours, but was able to wriggle forward efficiently. Soon the darkness closed in about her.

He cast about, and saw a long—handled flashlight on a nearby shelf. He grabbed it and shone it into the hole. Shree's tantalizing legs were still moving deep within it.

"Are you all right?" he called. "Got enough air?"

The feet paused. "Yes," her voice came back. "I am reaching a chamber." The feet resumed motion, then disappeared.

"I don't see you," Penn called, alarmed.

"I am standing in the chamber. It is not large, and seems to lead nowhere else."

"Then come on out of there. You may not be nervous, but I am."

"Yes." He knew she still had the band on her head, because she was merely communicating. Otherwise she might have laughed.

She came back out headfirst. He saw her in the light of the flash, but turned it off when the hanging blouse showed too much of her breasts. Anyway, he didn't want to blind her.

She reached the opening, and he helped her out. "Nothing in there?" he asked, disappointed.

"Nothing I was able to discover. This does seem curious. Why would there be a passage to nowhere?"

He pondered, and it came to him. "This house does not give up its secrets carelessly. There must be a key. Something to use or do to make that passage go somewhere. Just as there is to reach the attic."

"Perhaps the key is in the attic," she said.

"One of the devices we haven't figured out yet."

"Let me go there and read the inscriptions," she said. "If it is there, I will discover it."

They went upstairs, and to the attic. They saw no one else on the way; the others were probably involved in their own delvings.

Shree looked at the squiggle labels. "There is one that describes a—a—I am uncertain of the term for it. It seems to be a cube that is more than a cube, yet occupies the same space."

"A tesseract," he said. "A four dimensional cube."

"Yes, that seems to be the description. But this is not a device, but a switch. Shall I operate it?"

For a moment, Penn felt a qualm. But how were they going to learn anything if they didn't experiment? "Yes."

She switched it. Nothing happened. But that didn't necessarily mean anything. The answer should be in the cellar.

"I am rational, but my understanding is limited," Shree said as they descended. "Why should a switch for a thing in the cellar be in the attic? This does not seem convenient."

"I suspect it is not meant to be convenient," he said. "It may be dangerous, or significant, so the switch is hidden so that we must first discover the attic, then the cellar, as it were. A way of guaranteeing that we do not do things in the wrong order."

"Yes, now I understand. The inconvenience of crawling through the tunnel may be another such restriction."

Penn paused. "Would you remove the band for a moment, please?"

She removed it.

"How do you feel about this discovery?"

"I am strangely exhilarated. An extra-dimensional house prom-ses to be a remarkable experience. I am also mystified at how uch a thing can be. And somewhat concerned."

"Thank you. Those are my sentiments. Let's proceed cau-iously."

"Agreed." She donned the band again. "I still agree. I do not hink there is danger, but there could be mischief if we proceed 'ecklessly."

They passed the kitchen. Llynn and Chandelle were there, evi-lently preparing something. "Are you making progress?" Llynn ısked. "Because we aren't."

"We may be," Penn answered. "We'll soon know."

"Come back when you know," Chandelle said. "We're fixing a nack for the others."

They went on down. "Do you wish to take the flashlight?" Penn nquired.

"That might help," Shree agreed. "Perhaps I overlooked some-hing in the darkness."

She took the flashlight and crawled into the hole. This time Penn waited patiently, facing away from the tunnel. He was af-er all no teenager in need of sneaking peeks.

But after a time, the nervousness returned. "Shree!" he called. 'Everything okay?"

There was no answer.

Suddenly alarmed, he peered into the hole, but saw only dark-ness. He cast about for another flashlight, but saw none. He rushed upstairs.

"What's the matter?" Chandelle asked.

Penn hesitated. "Nothing, perhaps. I need a flashlight."

Chandelle fetched one. He took it and hurried away.

In the cellar, he shone the light into the tunnel. The light reached to the end and splashed against the far wall of the small chamber. It was empty.

Now he was really concerned. What had happened to Shree? Should he go in after her? But if there were danger there, surely it would affect him too. "Shree!" he called. "Where are you?"

Then she appeared in the chamber. "I am here," she called back.

He felt weak with relief. "I did not see you. That chamber must be bigger than it looks."

"In a manner. Let me join you, and explain." She crawled into the tunnel, and soon emerged at his end.

"When I called, and you didn't answer, I-was alarmed."

"I regret causing you distress. I was in what appears to be an alternate house."

"A house?"

"Perhaps another aspect of the tesseract. Another tube appeared, so I followed it, and found an empty house. But it had a device I have not seen in this one."

Penn was largely lost. "A device?"

"It appeared to be a control panel on the face of the—what you called the furnace."

"Maybe I had better take a look at it."

"As you wish. Follow me." She climbed back into the hole.

He gave her a moment, then climbed in after her. The fit was snug, but he was able to manage.

She got into the central chamber and stood there. He followed. There was just room for the two of them. Once again he was aware of her evocative body, so close. "Look," she said, gesturing.

He looked. There were two square holes where he had thought there was one. They were side by side, of equal size.

"The second one was not there before we went to the attic," she said. "The attic switch must have invoked it."

"But it's parallel to the first. Why didn't I see it from the cellar?"

"This appears to be the intersection point of the tesseract. Only one tunnel emerges in each house. The houses overlap."

"This I shall have to see."

"Follow me," she said again, and climbed into the second hole.

He followed. They emerged in the cellar, which looked the same as before. But when he turned around, there was just the one hole—and a bank of controls. It was a different furnace, or whatever it was.

Penn looked around the rest of the cellar. He saw the long flashlight lying on its shelf. The one he had given to Shree.

Except that she was still holding that flashlight. There were two of them. Plus the shorter one he held.

"Did you check upstairs?" he asked.

"No. I found the presence of this chamber, with you absent from it, sufficient. I returned immediately."

"Just as well," he said. "But let me check. I want to see if the rest of the house is empty."

He mounted the stairs and opened the door. The house was as before, in layout, but without furnishings. There also were no people in it. It was completely empty.

"An alternate house, of the tesseract," he said. "Unoccupied. We have indeed discovered something."

"That is my impression," Shree agreed.

"This must be the control bank for special adjustments, or whatever. The other house, the one we use, has just a mockup, the shape without the content."

"We'd better call in the others."

"I agree."

They returned to the cellar and navigated the tunnel. They emerged from the "second" one and entered the "first" one, going back. The cellar without the flashlight was there.

They went upstairs. Chandelle and Llynn were in the kitchen, with ice cream snacks for all. "We may have found it," Penn said.

That ushered in a day of considerable activity. Lloyd and Llynn set up before the control panel, while Chandelle and Shree reviewed the squiggle instructions by its dials and switches. Penn and Kailash became observers. This was not academic; they were constantly going back an forth.

"I think this is a fine tuner," Shree said. "A way to reset the defaults, so that we have full control of the house."

"Defaults?" Penn asked.

"Let me try one," Lloyd said. "This is for the front door. I'm setting it as far south as it will go. The screen shows nothing but snow."

Penn and Kailash crawled through the tunnels and back into the regular house. They went to the front door.

It opened onto a freezing landscape. "This must be Antarctica," Penn said.

"The panel by the door has no number," Kailash said.

"I suppose we can assign a number if we like the setting."

They returned to the alternate cellar. "Your screen is correct," Penn said. "It's sheer snow out there."

"Do we need to return to the other house to verify?" Kailash asked.

Surprised, Penn went to the front door of the alternate house. It, too, was set on snow. "No," he said. "Both aspects of the house move together."

"But you know, the house doesn't seem to be *at* any of the sites," Llynn said. "I wonder if we have it wrong?"

"You mean, like a computer?" Lloyd asked. "You think you're in a directory or folder or whatever, but actually it's just a convenience of labeling; everything's hopelessly mixed up on the hard disk."

"Yes. Maybe the house is in a state of—what's that newfangled stuff even Einstein couldn't understand?"

"Quantum physics," Penn said. "Where the position or speed of a particle isn't defined until you measure it."

"Yes, that nonsense," she said. "Suppose the house is like that?"

"Undefined until we set its doors?" Penn asked. "Could be. By choosing an address for a door, we orient the house on that site. The house itself is indefinite, in quantum uncertainty."

"It works for me," Lloyd said.

"But where does that leave *us*?" Llynn asked. "I mean, are we just patterns of nothing, until we leave the house?"

"Perhaps not nothing, but not what we seem to be," Penn said.

"I don't like that notion. That back door orients on time, not space, so it must be fixed, geographically. Maybe we can find out where it is, really, now."

"That won't tell us where the house is," Lloyd said. "It's just an address, like the front door."

"Then let's locate that address," she said impatiently. "I want to orient on *something*."

"She's got a point," Penn said.

"What point?" Lloyd demanded argumentatively. "With a computer, there *is* no—"

Shree put a hand on his shoulder. "Please," she murmured.

"On the way," Lloyd agreed instantly.

Penn was silent. The power of a woman was something to see. Fortunately Shree was using hers cautiously.

Lloyd did his magic on the screen, evoking an alignment of numbers. A map appeared, with bright spots indicating the zeroed in sites. One spot blinked. "There."

Penn focused on it. "Texas," he said. "South central. Close to Austin, I'd say."

"Now set the front door there," Llynn said.

Lloyd found the number, and set it. "Done."

Llynn stood. "I want to see it myself."

"I will go with you," Kailash said.

Chandelle caught Penn's eye warningly. "We'll all go," Penn said. If Llynn could get Kailash alone, and get him to kiss her, he saw no harm in it, but he didn't want an argument with his wife.

They went upstairs in House #2. The back door now opened on a city alley, for Lloyd had put in the present time. The front door opened in a street. "Come on, I want to see if we can walk around the house," Llynn said.

"But the rest of us should remain inside," Chandelle said. "To watch the doors."

So she wasn't quite as conservative as Penn had thought. He and Chandelle stood at the front door, and Lloyd and Shree were at the back door. Llynn and Kailash walked out the front. Penn saw them disappear. That made him nervous, though he was sure there was no actual danger.

In a minute there was a commotion at the back door. "They made it!" Lloyd exclaimed.

Then Llynn and Kailash walked into the living room from the back of the house. "We did it!" Llynn said, flushed with pleasure.

So they had a site in real time/space, for whatever it was worth. It was possible to align the doors. Probably it could be done for other sites. "Do you know, if we set the back door on Rome, we could study the history of the Roman Empire," Penn said, awed. "We couldn't change it, but we could see it outside our back door."

"This house remains amazing," Kailash said. "But we do not yet know its purpose."

"But we're getting there, maybe," Llynn said, hugging him.

"Perhaps," he agreed, though he looked uncertain about who was getting where. He had not encouraged Llynn's attention, but neither was he rejecting it.

"Maybe there's something new in this house's attic," Llynn said. "Come on!"

Kailash suffered himself to be dragged upstairs. The others remained downstairs.

Then Penn thought to look at the plaque by the stair. Sure enough, it had advanced to 9. Would 10 be the finale?

Chandelle looked out the back door. "This is nice, but I wish we could have a real forest, rather than a frozen one."

Lloyd perked up. "Bet we can do it, now. Fine tune it to a forest at the front door, and tie the back door in to that site. We don't have to stay here in the city."

"Let's do it," Penn said.

Penn, Lloyd, and Shree went to the cellar panel, while Chandelle went to make sure that Llynn and Kalash remained inside the house. Before long Lloyd had done it: the house was now on a site in British Columbia, Canada, in a forested valley by a long thin lake. There were no neighbors, and only a dirt road.

"Oh, lovely," Chandelle said, leading the way out. The house remained in view, the front and back doors aligned. They were in a glade, the water on one side, a forested slope on the other. There were birds in the trees, and a chipmunk watched them from a rock, before scurrying away. The air was fresh and warm.

Penn loved it too. Here they could use their hiking equipment, and camp out, without deserting the house. "I am really getting to like this house," he remarked.

"I like it too," Shree said.

"Yeah," Lloyd agreed immediately. "Want to go riding?"

She looked at Chandelle. Chandelle nodded. So the two of them went for the bicycles.

Penn looked at Chandelle. "No more chaperoning?"

"She is a responsible young woman, and his devotion gives her some reason to stay alive," she said. "I think that is more important than our limited conventions."

"You seem to be liberalizing."

"I think I am. I am falling in love with this house."

"I think we all are. I will hate to see the month end."

"We must make the most of it," she said. She took his hand, leading him through the high grass toward the water. "Do you think it's warm enough to swim?"

"It may be. But we didn't bring our suits."

She just looked at him. Then he realized just how far the house had liberalized her. Not only was she enjoying the countryside, when she had before been more of a city creature, she was acting much as she had during their courtship, forty years before. Then they had skinny dipped, and more.

And if the young folk found them, well they could swim too.

Chapter 11
Alien Dream

Llynn lay on her bed, toying with the fiber ring she had found n the attic. That had been the only new thing, apart from the esseract switch Shree had found, and the squiggle instructions uggested merely that it was a sleeping aid, or at least that it rought interesting dreams. It showed a person wearing it, then ying down, and seeing all manner of things and creatures. So he was trying it, though she was disappointed. The controls in he cellar of the alternate house had given them significant ad-litional control of the residence. It would have been reasonable or the attic to provide similarly. But it hadn't.

Shree was lying on her bed. She removed the gray band from ier head.

"How are you doing?" Llynn asked.

"I am mending. Having accepted the notion that your culture loes not regard me as worthy only of death, I am finding it easier o believe. But there is a problem."

Llynn had been afraid of that. "Will you tell me? I can keep a secret."

"It is no secret. It is that after your month is done, you will eave this house, and my brother and I will have nowhere to go."

Llynn hadn't thought of that. "But you could stay with the iouse."

"We have no resources. We would not be able to pay its rental."

"Then you could step out in America with us."

"We are undocumented aliens. Your country has restrictions on illegal immigrants. In any event, we would have no jobs and no residences there. It does not seem feasible. I am a millstone around my brother's neck, and I will bear him down with me if I remain with him."

Llynn hadn't thought of any of that. "But you're a wonderful woman. Lloyd would be heartbroken if you—" She broke off, not wanting to speak of death.

"Were your cousin of age, I might marry him, and become a citizen. But he is not, and in any event it would not be fair to him."

Llynn sat up on the bed. "Shree, if you snapped your fingers, he would walk through fire for you. How could it be unfair?"

"He is not of age to judge well. It is merely his inexperience that foolishly captivates him."

Llynn couldn't accept that. "Shree, if I were a boy, I'd be in love with you. You're so beautiful. As it is—"

"You love my brother. Yet you, too, must separate from him when the month is done."

It was true. Lloyd would have to go back to his family in Okinawa, and Llynn to hers in Philadelphia. This phenomenal experience would have to end, when the month did. "Damn it!" she swore. "It's not fair."

"I apologize for dismaying you."

"And you're thinking of dying! That's part of it."

"It is true."

Llynn fixed on another aspect. "Maybe I could go with Kailash to your country."

"You would not be well equipped for that life."

She was right. In fact it was an understatement. What little she had learned of the Himalyan region of northern India, of Kashmir, suggested that it was a lot rougher than the cashmere sweaters it exported. She was totally unequipped. All avenues seemed blocked.

Then she became cunning. "If all is lost at the end of the month, I want to make what I can of it. Shree—"

Shree stood. "Yes, I will bring him. This much I can do for you." She left the room, making no noise.

She understood! Llynn's heart beat wildly. She knew that what she contemplated was wrong, but it was what she wanted. She had always been wild, and the wildness was returning.

The door opened, and Kailash entered, wearing pajamas. He did not speak, but came to sit beside her on the bed. She turned into him and embraced him, her mouth seeking his. She kissed him hungrily.

He returned the kiss. But then he drew back. "I do not wish to violate the hospitality of this house, or of your grandparents," he said. "I like you, Llynn, very much, and would like to do this with you. But in the present circumstances, it would be wrong."

"I don't care!" she flared. "I love you."

"And perhaps I love you. But I would not be the man you think me to be if I took advantage of your distress in this manner. Sleep, Llynn, and I will sleep too—in the other bed."

Something else occurred to her. "Shree's with Lloyd."

"Yes, in similar manner."

"It must be nice, having adult honor," she said, frustrated.

"It is often painful."

She knew there would be no arguing with him. Part of her was relieved. "Okay. You take the other bed. But if you change your mind, you're welcome."

"Thank you." He got up and walked to the other bed.

Llynn lay down again. She still held the fiber ring. She put it on her middle finger, so as not to lose it, and closed her eyes.

The dreams started immediately. She felt herself expanding, becoming diffuse, spreading beyond the house and beyond the city. Then beyond the planet, and the solar system. She became a galactic phenomenon, embracing a hundred million stars and encompassing the colossal engine that drove the galaxy, the central black hole.

Frightened by the immensity, she withdrew. She contracted back to her sector, her system, her world, her region, her house, her body. "Oh!"

Kailash was there, concerned. "You are uncomfortable?"

"I—I was dreaming. But it was so big—as big as all the galaxy. I couldn't handle it."

"The ring," he said. "It sponsors this?"

She had forgotten the ring. "Yes, I guess it does. It's powerful!"

"Perhaps you should remove it."

She considered. "No. Maybe I should find out just what it's doing. That dream was going somewhere. I just got scared, not realizing that it wasn't really *my* dream."

"As you wish. I do not wish to interfere."

She gazed at the ring on her finger. "Kailash—would you—?"

"I will stay with you while you dream," he agreed. "I will hold your hand."

"Thank you." She gave him her hand as he sat on her bed, and he took it and held it. She savored the moment, then closed her eyes and relaxed.

The dream came rushing. She expanded again to galactic status. But she felt her hand, far behind, held by the gentle pressure of Kailash's fingers. That reassured her; she had not lost touch with reality.

Now she became aware of other dream bubbles. They overlapped hers, having different centers. They were mental entities, seeking others of their kind. Some were male, some female, some neuter, some indeterminate. Some were young, some old. Some were familiar, some strange, some utterly weird.

She oriented on those that were most like her. Young, female, willful, adventurous. These presences firmed. She focused further, looking for one who was balked in passion.

There was one. *Salutation*, the alien female said.

"Hello. Who are you?"

"I am ★∇Ω‡¿. Who are you."

"I am Llynn Wiley, of Planet Earth. I have not been here before."

"This is my third time. Do you wish to exchange?"

"I don't know. What is it?"

You will visit my body, and I will visit yours.

"Visit each other's bodies? Is this possible?"

★∇Ω‡¿ made something like a laugh. *Yes. This is why we meet ere. To enable compatible temporary exchanges.*

"Is there any danger?"

Not when it is agreed. We each split our minds, so that part emains behind to assist the visitor. It ends the moment either visi- or withdraws.

"Sounds interesting."

Yes. That is why we do it. It is a considerable diversion from motional pain.

"You are hurting?"

I wish to receive the seed of a favored person, but she is lost.

"She? I thought you were female."

Yes. We are all female. You are not?

"I am female, but wish to—to receive the seed of a male."

Your species has two genders!

"Yes. Yours doesn't?"

Mine does not, ★∇Ω‡¿ agreed.

"But then how can you reproduce?"

We fetch in each other's signals, and invoke the regenerative ortions. It must be fascinating to do it with two genders.

"Yes. But I don't understand how you 'fetch in' those signals."

Then we must exchange, and you may learn how it is done. That is always best.

"Okay, if it's safe."

I will guide you, as you have not exchanged before. Then you will comprehend, and so will I.

"Okay. How do we exchange?"

Merge with me, and follow me to my home. I will also follow ou. We will remain in touch.

"Okay." Llynn found that she knew how to merge; it was sim- ly a matter of overlapping completely, so that their mental centers unified. She became ★∇Ω‡¿, and the alien became Llynn Wiley.

★∇Ω‡¿ shrank, and Llynn with her. She coalesced on a portion of a windy planet, on the steep bare slope of a mountain, anchored by her one foot. Other creatures were spaced around her, similarly anchored. All were combing the air with their web antennae.

"This is you?" Llynn asked, not quite as surprised as she would have been if awake.

Yes. This is my life.

"Weird."

And this fleshly casing is your life?

Llynn returned her awareness to her own body, back on Earth. "Yes. Maybe I'd better introduce you to my companion, Kailash. He is a male of my species."

Phenomenal! How do you communicate?

"We speak. Maybe I'd better do it, the first time, so you can learn how. Note what I do."

I am noting.

Llynn took over her vocal cords and spoke. "Kailash."

He squeezed her hand. "Yes, Llynn."

"I am in contact with an alien being from a distant world. Her name is ★∇Ω‡¿. She is visiting my body for a while, and would like to meet you."

Kailash had the grace to take it in stride. "Hello, Staromega."

Both Llynn and ★∇Ω‡¿ laughed at the way he mangled the alien name. "We lack the means to speak your name correctly," Llynn explained. "He means no offense."

I will attempt to speak to him, ★∇Ω‡¿ thought. She assumed control of the vocal system and said "Hll, Klsh."

"That is close enough," he said with a smile.

Is it? ★∇Ω‡¿ asked Llynn.

"Not really. You have symbols for the vowel sounds. It should be hEllO,KAIlAsh."

Weird, ★∇Ω‡¿ thought, echoing Llynn. Then she tried again. "Hello, Kailash." There was a strong alien accent, but it was intelligible.

"Much better," he agreed. "What can I do for you?"

"Demonstrate your breeding process."

He paused, perhaps suspecting that Llynn was teasing him. "That is not immediately feasible. But I will describe it to you, if you wish."

"It would be easier to demonstrate it," ★∇Ω‡¿ said. "My assimilation of your strange sonic communication is imperfect."

Kailash paused again. "Is there a way to verify your identity?"

"Touch my appendage." ★∇Ω‡¿ raised Llynn's hand.

He touched her fingers. There was an almost electric pulse. "Completely alien," he said, amazed.

Llynn took her mouth. "I told you."

"Then perhaps you should tell Staromega why I may not honor her request."

"*You* tell her. As far as I'm concerned, demonstration is easier." Llynn was enjoying this.

Am I encountering alien foibles? ★∇Ω‡¿ asked.

Kailash tackled it. "Let me explain something. In our species, reproduction is not casually performed. There are formidable associated commitments. There is a requirement that both parties be of sufficient age, and your host is not. So though a demonstration would be physically possible, it is not socially feasible. But I will clarify the process verbally, if you wish."

"That will suffice," ★∇Ω‡¿ agreed verbally.

"I'm getting out of here," Llynn said, disgusted. She reverted to the alien host body. She did this by a quick expansion to universe size, and contraction on the other body, knowing the way now, as they remained connected.

She was back on the mountain slope, combing the air. Suddenly she made a connection: "Barnacle! I'm a barnacle. Seining the water for food, only it's not water but air." This realization helped her orient. She combed for nourishment, sliding it down to her mouth, which was used only for eating.

But there was more than food coming in on the wind. There was information. It came in tiny packets of molecules, like spores, and she assimilated their messages even as she digested them. Each packet identified its originator, another creature like ★∇Ω‡¿, but with a different flavor. She was part of a community, and felt comfort in the ambiance.

She realized that she wasn't actually looking around, because she had no eyes. Her mesh antenna served instead, reading the wind; she interpreted it as seeing, but was aware only of the things upwind. Downwind seemed not to exist.

This was a good day for food; the wind was loaded with it. It consisted of rock dust stirred in trace amounts from the mountain, and plant pollen, though what grew here was not exactly of the plant kingdom. But food could be assimilated without thought. Life could get dull, in the summer season, which was of course why ★∇Ω‡¿ had sought intellectual adventure in the galaxy.

Then something special arrived. It was an information packet, with a pattern that aroused her extreme interest. What was it?

Well, she would ask. "★∇Ω‡¿," she called. But there was no answer.

So after a moment she switched back to Earth. This time she did it slowly, just for variety, as this whole alien contact was a novel experience for her. She expanded to match the size of the mountain—and saw, or rather sensed, something odd. There was a shape like a huge green rug crawling up and across the mountain, covering many of the barnacles. What was it?

Very well: that made two things to ask about. She increased her expansion, and flickered huge and then small, and was back at her human body.

★∇Ω‡¿ was kissing Kailash, and pressing her body—Llynn's body—against him.

Llynn took over her head and jerked it back. "What's going on ere?" she demanded.

"Llynn—you're back," Kailash said, looking abashed.

"Just in time, too, by the look of it," she said severely. "★∇Ω‡¿—what are you doing?"

I am getting him to demonstrate, the alien female replied.

"You're doing more than that. You're seducing him."

Yes. We ascertained that I am after all of age, as I have reproduced before. Therefore when the sonic description became tedious—

"Well, forget it. It's my body. If anybody's going to seduce him, t's me."

"There will be no seduction," Kailash said, blushing.

She looked at him. "Not now. You thought you'd grab some alien tail?"

"It was merely to show the preliminary—"

"And she was taking you to the finale." But Llynn did not feel comfortable sounding like Grandma. She knew she was just jealous of the alien's rapid success where Llynn herself had failed. Obviously sexual expertise cut across the barrier of species, and even a unisex barnacle could learn it swiftly. So she got back on he subject. "★∇Ω‡¿, I have two questions. What is the rug that's climbing the mountain? And—"

A rug?

Llynn made a mental picture. "Green, downwind of us. Rather pretty, but I wondered."

That is a ≡≡≡! ★∇Ω‡¿ thought with horror.

"That's bad?"

A terrible predator. It grazes on our kind. I must return to thwart it.

"I'll go with you," Llynn said. And, to Kailash: "And don't get fresh with my body while we're gone." For she knew that with both of them devoting full attention to ★∇Ω‡¿'s body, no one would be minding the store here.

"Of course I will not," he agreed.

They expanded and contracted, and were there. *All seems well* ★∇Ω‡¿ thought. *How did you detect the ≡≡≡?*

"I did a slow expansion, and I guess I overlapped it."

I never thought of that. We must verify.

They expanded together. There was the green rug, slightly closer.

They shrank back to the body. *I think your warning has just saved my life,* ★∇Ω‡¿ thought. *Now I must become repulsive.*

"Repulsive?"

To taste bad to the ≡≡≡, so it won't graze me. ★∇Ω‡¿ concentrated, generating a special type of discharge. Llynn had not realized that her body had been putting out gas and particles, but it must have, because she had been tuning in on the emissions of the barnacles upwind.

That starts it, ★∇Ω‡¿ thought after a moment. *Those downwind of me will receive it, and do likewise, and the monster will be repelled. Thanks to your warning.*

"Are you sure? I wouldn't want you to get eaten."

We can verify, using your device. They did a partial expansion. Sure enough, the green rug was now retreating.

They relaxed, recovering from the scare. *I apologize for trying to seduce your male. I did not realize you would object.*

"That's all right," Llynn said. "I was just jealous. When I tried it, he wouldn't touch me. How did you do it?"

I pretended to be hopelessly confused by his sonic description. When he spoke of holding digits, I made him demonstrate on your hand. When he spoke of touching mouths together—

"I get the picture," Llynn said. "Easy stages. I should have thought of that. Men can be led, when they don't know what's going on."

That is my impression. The male format is delightful. I regret that we did not have time to—

"Well, as he said, we have conventions."

What was your other question?

"Oh. I caught this interesting packet, and wondered—"

That is an ideal breeding formula! In fact, this is the one I was ooking for, that I thought lost.

"A what?"

We reproduce only when we encounter a perfect complemen-ary match to our own formula. Because each individual is differ-nt, such matches do not occur often. I must make an offspring.

"Uh, do I need to go?"

No, there is no privacy about it. I will simply match this pattern vith my own, and form flesh around it, and anchor it beside me. will forage for it, until it is able to do that alone. It will gradu-lly move into new territory and become an individual entity. This s how we spread into regions denuded by the ≡≡≡. It takes time, ut we have much of that.

"How do you move, with only one anchored foot?"

We extend a toe on one side, and retract one on the far side. This oo takes time, but—

"I know. You have plenty. Your lifestyle seems sort of slow paced o me."

Yours seems very hurried. It is a refreshing contrast. Your mode f breeding with differently constructed males is most intriguing. would like to learn more of it.

"Well, come back and learn," Llynn said. "Maybe this time I an seduce him."

I regret I must not. I must focus on the construction of my own ffspring, lest I lose the formula again. But I am glad I encoun-tered you, Earth alien creature. It has been most interesting.

It was a clear enough dismissal. "We'll have to do it again some-time," Llynn said. "I'll go home now. Bye, ★∇Ω‡¿."

Peaceful separation, Llll.

Llynn expanded and contracted, and returned to her own body. The contact faded out. Her alien dream was over, but she had much to think about.

She opened her eyes. Kailash was there, sitting beside her su-pine body. "Okay, I'm back," she said. "Now, if you like—"

He got up quickly and moved to the other bed. "This appears to have been a most interesting experience for you. In the morning you must tell the family every detail."

She smiled. "*Almost* every detail."

He nodded. "That is perhaps best."

"I guess I don't have a chance to seduce you now."

"That is correct."

"What was it like, when she tried?"

"She is more experienced than you, in the—the wiles. She had a peculiar intensity. At first I did not realize what she intended and when I did, I no longer cared. Had you not returned—"

"Yeah. But you know, I saved her life, because I found a predator coming after her. She's okay now, but she wouldn't have been. So it worked out okay."

"I am glad the experience was satisfactory."

"Yeah. I'll never disparage a barnacle again."

"A barnacle?"

"That's what she resembles, physically. They're different, but ★∇Ω‡¿ was a person. A girl, like me, in spirit."

"Much like you," he agreed.

Llynn liked that. "Oh, hell, come and lie with me, Kailash. Just to sleep. I promise I won't try anything."

"I am uncertain that this is wise."

"Please. I promise."

He hesitated a moment more, then surrendered. He came to share her bed.

"Put your arm over me," she said.

He lay on his side and put his arm carefully over her waist. She turned into him, snuggled her hair against his chin, and relaxed. "This is heaven," she murmured, and drifted into sleep.

Chapter 12
Man of the House

Lloyd put the leash on Obsidian and took her out the back loor. The frozen forest had become somewhat stale for the rest of them, but the dog always found a new aspect to sniff. Only it vas no longer frozen; he remembered as he saw the edge of the ake. This was live, thanks to the fine tuning. In fact they had seen the old folk skinny-dipping, but not had the nerve to join hem. Anyway, it had been so great bike riding with Shree, nothng else mattered. She had seemed to enjoy it too, though they had had to get off frequently and walk past rough spots; she hadn't out the headband on the whole time.

They had been in this house only a week or so, but he knew heir adventure was coming to an end. They had explored just about every aspect of the house, and made it change its settings and all, and they were on the brink of catching on to the last of it. Then the fun would be over. Oh, they might stay through the nonth, but then they would have to leave, because it really wasn't heir house. It was just on loan to them, and they had no other claim on it.

But returning to home and school in Okinawa, and being a military brat again, promised to be truly dull. He wanted to stay here in this house, and range the world, with Grandpa Penn and Grandma Chandelle and Cousin Llynn, and with Kailash and Shree. Especially Shree. What was going to become of her? If he could, he would marry her; but he couldn't, for so many reasons. But he didn't much want to live without her.

They returned to the house. Shree was there, standing at the door. "Hello, Lloyd," she said.

"Hi, Shree." He was always halfway tongue-tied in her presence. Adults thought that instant love was impossible, and that thirteen was too young, but he knew better. He was caught in it and loving the fact of it, even though he knew that she was merely being polite to him.

"May I talk with you?" she asked.

"Sure. Anytime."

"Outside?"

"Okay." As if he could ever tell her no, on anything.

They moved along the lake, and sat on a warm ledge of exposed rock just out of sight of the house, with Obsidian happily lying at their feet. Lloyd waited, thrilled to have her attention, whatever the reason.

She took a deep breath, and spoke. "Lloyd, you know I have no future. I can't leave the environs of this house, and if I could, I would have to leave the reconciler behind." She removed the gray band from her head and held it loosely in her hand. "I can endure without it for brief periods, but not for extended ones. I also could not do well without the translator." She touched her fine ear, reminding him that she was speaking in her language, and he in his. "So I may choose to die, and even if I wished to live, I have nowhere to go."

Lloyd forced himself to speak. "I know."

"So when happens what happens, that will be too late to speak to you. So I choose this time. I wish to thank you for your effort in rescuing me from my horror, and to say that even were I not indebted to you, I would like you for yourself. I enjoyed yesterday's companionship, riding along the lake. I am able to exist without the reconciler longer in your presence than elsewhere."

A warm shiver ran over him. "You don't have to say that, Shree. You know I'm just a—"

"And you know what I am," she said. "Yet you truly like me. Your feeling is unconditional."

"Yeah." What else could he say? She had this cultural thing

that she was unclean, because of what they had made her do. He didn't care at all about that, but he was just a kid whose opinion hardly counted. She was so beautiful!

"And so I wish to give you this, in friendship," she said. "For no other reason."

"Oh, I don't want to take anything you need."

She smiled. "This I can spare."

"Oh. Okay." He was being awkward, as usual.

She turned to him, and lifted her hands to his head, thrilling him with her fine touch. She brought her divine face to his, and kissed him on the mouth, softly but firmly. Lloyd thought he was going to faint. There was nothing in the world but the rapture of her lips on his.

Then she ended it, but remained for a moment, holding his head in her hands. "This is as much as I can give you," she said. "But I give it gladly. Lloyd, in my fashion, I love you."

Then he did faint.

An eternity and a moment later, he swam back to consciousness. Shree had her arms around him, holding him close. Heaven extended!

Obsidian was nosing him, jealous of the attention. He moved a hand just enough to stroke her soft ears.

"Are you all right?" Shree asked, sounding concerned.

"I'm great," he breathed. "What you said—I know you mean it figuratively, but still it put me into—into—"

"Nirvana," she said. "I know you love me, Lloyd. I am not free to love you back in the way you might wish, but I would not hurt you for all the world."

"Oh. You love me like a sister," he said, descending some distance from heaven, but still extremely grateful for her caring.

"No. Like a lover. The barriers between us are your age and my unworthiness. In time you will be older, and in time I would be able to live without the reconciler. But those require perhaps years, and we have less than a month. But I am as grateful for your feeling, which cleanses me, as I am for the way you rescued me, and so I love you to the extent I am able. More there cannot be."

Heaven was tantalizingly close again. "Oh, Shree, I wish—"

"I will kiss you once more. Then I think it must not be again. But you will know."

"I will know," he echoed. He was in infinite bliss, and infinite sadness. If this was the renowned pain of love, he understood it all too well.

She kissed him, and held him close while he recovered. Then she gently let him go. She brought out a comb and combed his mussed hair, and used a handkerchief to clean his smudged face. She adjusted his shirt, putting him in order. By these tokens she let him know that this was to be their secret. He wished he could remain forever, being tended by her.

But she had given him her message, and it was time to go. They stood, and followed the lake, returning to the house. With that entry, things returned to normal, with Chandelle in the kitchen, and the others stirring. But Lloyd knew that he would never return to his prior being. He had tasted heaven, or nirvana, and if there was never any more, it would last his lifetime.

He went to his room and sat on his bed, letting his head clear. Shree had actually spent the night there, so as to let her brother be with Llynn, but she had remained on the other bed and made no advances to him. She had saved that for the boulder outside. But he—what was he to do? His snotty past existence had been rendered forever obsolete.

And within a month, she would die. He understood the ineluctable logic of it. Their relationship was dependent on the house, and they would have to leave the house when they finished their month.

The enormity of that coming loss overwhelmed him. He lay face down on the bed and cried.

After a time he turned over, in mood as well as in body. Did it really have to end? Why *couldn't* they stay in the house? Oh, sure, he had to return to Okinawa, and Llynn had to go home to Philadelphia, but the grandparents could live where they chose, and if they chose this house, Kailash and Shree could stay with them, couldn't they? The house knew no boundaries; it had no nationality. There was a time limit of a month, sure, but that was just the rent-free time. After that they would have to pay. They figured they couldn't afford it, but that was because they didn't have a lot of money. Suppose the rent wasn't money?

Seized by a notion, he went to the computer cubby and turned on the system. He didn't know what he was searching for, but sometimes his thinking was facilitated by surfing the Net. He got online and cruised, heedless of where he was going, just trying to catch on to the lurking idea that played just beyond his consciousness. What other rent could there be, except money?

He got nowhere. The house connected to the Net, but the Net didn't connect to the house. All the information in the world, except what he most wanted to know. But, damn it, there had to be something, somewhere, somehow.

Chandelle came to call him to breakfast. The day was still early, though so much had already happened. He shut down and went. They ate as a family now, with Chandelle serving. Llynn sat beside Kailash, and by default Lloyd sat beside Shree. She looked perfectly composed. Girls were good at that.

"Are you all right, dear?" Chandelle inquired.

What use to try to lie? "No. I've been thinking about the house. End of the month we'll have to leave, and that means—"

Penn nodded. "That means we all go home, except Shree."

Shree put on the reconciler. "I will manage," she said. "I can exist as an undocumented alien."

"Doing what?" Llynn asked sharply.

Shree removed the headband. "It is true. I do not wish to do that again." Understatement of the century, Lloyd thought.

"There has to be another alternative," Chandelle said.

"What we need is to stay in this house," Lloyd said. "All of us, or at least everyone over seventeen."

"I don't think we can do that," Penn said.

"Why not? I don't think this house wants money. It must have cost more than we'll ever see just to build it."

"True. Any rental would be a mere token. But I very much doubt that we would be able to meet any other requirements."

"The house summoned us," Llynn said. "It wants us. We just don't know why."

"And that's what I'm trying to figure out," Lloyd said. "If we knew why it wants us, we'd know whether we can stay. I'll bet that tenth level on the plaque is for when we figure that out."

Penn nodded again. "Your grandmother and I have discussed this. We suspect that we might be better off not figuring that out. Perhaps leaving before the month is done."

"But then—"

"True. We can't leave like that. It isn't just Shree. None of us can leave without knowing the answer to the riddle of this house."

"But we fear it's a trap," Chandelle said. "Too much has been offered."

"But it's great stuff!" Lloyd said.

Llynn was sharper. "What do you mean, too much?"

"We don't wish to alarm you," Penn said, evidently ill at ease.

Now Lloyd knew there was something serious. "Too much what?"

Penn sighed. "There are the material things, of course. It's a very nice house, with very nice accommodations. The television, the computer, the books and equipment."

"The undo buttons," Llynn agreed.

"The traveling doors," Lloyd said. "The attic full of toys. What's your point?"

When Penn still hesitated, Kailash spoke. "I believe he means us. Shree and me."

Lloyd felt a chill, this time not a nice one. "You two are offerings?"

"Hostages," Llynn said grimly.

The chill deepened. "You mean, the house didn't want you two for yourselves, but to use against us? We gotta do what it wants, or we lose you?"

"This is our concern," Kailash agreed. "We are dependent on the acceptance of the house."

It did make tough sense. "But what does it want?"

Now Shree spoke. "We think it wants your family to remain. If you do not, we are lost."

"Remain for *what*?"

"We do not know," she said sadly. "But we fear for your welfare. There is enormous power associated with this house, so what it desires can hardly be anything minor."

"But we want to stay anyway," Lloyd said. "At least I do. I love it here. It doesn't need to force me."

"Or me," Llynn said.

"We like it too," Chandelle said. "It seems to be a perfect retirement residence."

"Therefore, chances are that the price is extremely steep," Penn said. "Something we will not want to pay, unless under the duress of forfeiting the lives of two we have come to value, and perhaps to love."

Lloyd saw Llynn nod. She loved Kailash. And he loved Shree. "You mean, like giving up our kidneys or eyeballs?"

Penn shook his head. "I doubt it, considering the formidable healing powers of its artifacts."

"Then *what*?" Lloyd repeated.

There was a pause. Then, with evident reluctance, Penn spoke. "We do not know. But we suspect something like a captive breeding program."

"Captive breeding!" Llynn exclaimed. "So aliens can have human babies to experiment on?"

"Or to raise as aliens," Chandelle said. "To become human aliens. The way we raise hunting dogs or beasts of burden."

"Oh, God," Llynn breathed. "So they took us young, so we can breed a lot, while the older folk feed and clothe us. A puppy mill."

Kailash shook his head. "Yet with only two couples, the variety as well as the number would be severely limited. They would do better to steal existing babies."

"That could stir up trouble among the natives," Penn said. "They might require only four combinations for their purposes."

"Or six," Chandelle said tightly.

Lloyd was baffled. "I see two. I don't see four or six."

"I fear I do," Kailash said. "Cousin with cousin. Brother with sister."

Now he got it. "And grandfather with granddaughter, and with—"

"With me," Shree said. "Three males, two young females. Six viable combinations for the laboratory."

"If they don't have a way to make old females young," Chandelle said, looking pained. "It is also possible that they would have incubation for reduced term babies, so as to be able to produce them every couple of months."

"Queen ants," Llynn said, shuddering. "I see what you mean about a steep price."

Lloyd couldn't face it. "But we don't know that! We're just guessing."

Shree looked at him with softness and pity. "It is a guess that answers the question well. We may accept it, if we wear the reconcilers."

Lloyd had a wild notion. "If so, if that's it, and we've figured it out, then that plaque will stand at 10 now. So we can check."

The others nodded agreement. But no one moved.

Lloyd realized that it was up to him. "Okay, I'll look." He dragged himself up.

He walked to the plaque and forced himself to look, fearing what he would see.

The number was 9.

"It's okay!" he yelled. "It hasn't turned! It's nine."

Then the rest of them were with him, clustering around, read-ng the number for themselves. "Thank God," Penn said.

"But there must be a reason," Llynn said. "Maybe just as bad."

"We do have to know," Chandelle said. "Before we decide."

"I think we had better do some serious thinking," Penn said. "All of us."

No one argued.

Lloyd retreated to his room. After a moment Shree joined him. "I am sorry," she said. "These are ugly conjectures."

"Yeah. But how do we come up with better ones?"

"I thought perhaps you would wish to try the aliens."

"What?"

"Llynn visited with aliens, by using the ring she found in the alternate attic. Here it is." She proffered a fiber ring. "She thought I would want to try it next, but I think you may do better with it."

Lloyd took the ring. It seemed ordinary, except that it wasn't made of metal. It was more like something woven of heavy fi-ber. "You want me to try this?"

"I do not mean to urge you to anything you prefer not to do," she said quickly. "I will try it." She reached for the ring.

"No, I'll do it. How does it work?"

"Llynn put it on her finger and lay down. She said it was like a dream. Kailash remained with her, to be sure there was no trouble."

"Oh, I thought he was there to—"

"No. No more than I with you. But she said she made contact with an alien female who took her body and tried to seduce him."

"Scary!"

"No, the alien meant well. She was nice, Llynn said. But she also told me that if I tried it, I should have someone with me, just in case."

"And not your brother."

She blushed. Answer enough. He was glad she wasn't wearing

the reconciler band now, for that would have squelched any such emotion.

He looked at the ring again, intrigued. If an alien male came and wanted to make out with a human female, would Shree le it? "This visitation—what happens to the original person?"

"It was a voluntary exchange. Both minds were there, when they wanted to be; they shared. Llynn said it was a great experience, and she wants to do it again. But there is only one ring, so she is letting others try it now."

"I'll try it. You think maybe there's an answer out there? About the house?"

"It is possible."

"Will you sit with me and hold my hand?"

"Yes, Lloyd."

"I'm on my way." He jammed the ring on his middle finger and lay back on the bed. Shree sat beside him and took his other hand.

He felt himself expanding. It was like a computer screen zooming into a view of the globe of the Earth from space. But this went farther, right on to the galactic scale.

Then he became aware of other presences. Some were male, like himself. Some were female. Some were neuter. They were all ages and types. So he focused on one like himself: juvenile and bratty and in love.

I share your pain, the alien thought.

"You're too young to marry her?"

Marry?

"To breed with her?"

Breed?

"For some stupid reason, you can't be with her?"

Exactly. Do you have a solution?

"No, I'm looking for one."

Unfortunate. The alien drifted on.

So much for that. So he oriented on a young female. "Hi,

sweetie,"

You are looking for alien romance?

"Not really. Just some advice."

What kind of creature are you, physically?

That stumped him for a moment. So he got basic. "Flesh and blood. Land walker. Air breather."

Ugh! she thought, repulsed.

"Yeah? What's your body like?"

Sublime slime.

She was serious. "You're right. I'm not your type." He drifted on.

This time an alien focused on him. *I note that you rejected an appealing female. I am a male of romantic persuasion.*

"No thanks!" Lloyd didn't even inquire about the physical nature of this entity.

He contracted himself back to his own planet and body, and opened his eyes. "Hello, lovely alien creature."

Shree laughed. "How was it, Lloyd?"

"Not as great as being with you."

"Thank you. You found no answer?"

He pondered, not wanting to admit failure. And it came to him, in a phenomenal flash. "I think I've got it!"

"You have it?"

"Alien exchanges. They're haphazard. But if they were organized—I think that's it. That's why they let us have the alien contact ring at this point."

"I don't understand."

"Come on! I gotta bounce this off the whole family, and see if the number turns." He jumped up and half dragged her along after him.

Soon they were all assembled around the kitchen table. "Yes, Lloyd," Penn said.

"I was trying the alien dreamer ring," he said, twisting it off his finger. "I expanded real big, and met three aliens, but none of them were right. And I thought that must be a problem. Like these lonely hearts ads on the Internet or newspaper, all these men looking, and women looking, and chances are they gotta try a lot of others, and it still doesn't work out, because they just don't know enough about each other. But if they had a better framework, like a tourist attraction, or if they're bored and just want to travel without a big hassle, or running into someone who just wanted to grope them psychically—a good setup might be really popular. Like going on a cruise, where everything's planned, and they don't have to worry about the details. Only this is interplanetary."

"Alien tourist trade?" Llynn asked dubiously.

"Yeah! And Earth is just one port, one stop out of thousands they can choose. See the sights, stare at the natives, buy novelties, have fun. Betcha there's a big market."

Penn nodded. "A tourist station. For aliens to visit safely. But how could they breathe the air, or eat the food, if their metabolism is completely different?"

"Not physically!" Llynn said, catching on. "Mentally. They come to share the mind. See through the native's eyes, hear through his ears, eat through his mouth, and all. And if they get confused, the native will explain things for them; he's right there too, or he can go if they want to be alone. They can be friends, exchanging planets for a while, getting to know each other. It's nice."

"Right," Lloyd said. "Maybe it's our bodies they want to use, not to take over, not to breed with, just to ride with for a while. To have a weird experience. Tourists."

"Tourists," Penn echoed. "With trained natives, to facilitate things. To run the local shop, since they can't readily send aliens here physically. You are sure it's voluntary?"

"Yes," Lloyd and Llynn said together. Then Llynn added "At least, the alien dream ring is. You're in control, and you can opt out anytime. And it is fun, like a game."

"Like an on-line chat room," Lloyd said. "Only bigger, and you an share bodies right away."

"And you *can* breed, or at least have—" Llynn faltered. "Ro-nance. In the native's body. If it's okay with the host."

"Some tourists would like that," Chandelle said.

Penn nodded. "Then let's look at the plaque."

They went to the plaque. It had turned to 10.

"Next question," Penn said. "Do we want to do this?"

"Yes," Lloyd and Llynn said together again.

Penn looked at Kailash. "Yes, this would be an ideal situation," Kailash said.

"I would be glad to remain in this house, and meet alien minds," Shree said. "It is far superior to my alternatives."

Penn looked at Chandelle. "We need to know more," she said. "But if this really is the point of this house, I would be amenable."

"So would I," Penn said. "How do we negotiate with the aliens?"

"How many cubes are there in a tesseract?" Kailash asked.

"I'm not sure that has been defined. Perhaps four, overlapping each other. Perhaps an infinite number."

"Then there must be more to this house than the two chambers we have seen. I suspect that the way to the third house is now open."

"Let's go," Lloyd said, leading the way.

They trooped to the cellar, and through the tunnels to the second house. Now there was a second tunnel beside the first, departing from that house. Lloyd led the way through that, turned in the small chamber, and wriggled on out to the cellar.

He knew immediately that it was different. There were things on the shelves, and a carpet on the floor. "Bingo," he said as Shree emerged behind him.

When they were all assembled there, they went cautiously up the stairs and opened the door. This house was furnished, but not at all like the first one. It was crafted to satisfy a different taste. Lloyd had the feeling they were intruding.

They entered the living room. A man was just getting out c his chair. He was middle aged, balding, and heavyset: unprepos sessing except for his presence here. "Hello, family," he said. " know you. I am Abner, the man of the house. Sit down and w shall talk."

Somewhat taken aback, they spread out around the room an took seats. Lloyd was glad that Shree chose to sit next to him.

"You have graduated from the course in excellent time," Abne said. "You understand the nature and purpose of this house. Yo are correct: it is to be a tourist station, for visitors from acros the galaxy who prefer the ease of a prepackaged tour. You mus be prepared to host alien entities in your minds, and to shov them the quaint aspects of the local planet. But the control o your bodies will always be yours, and you may decline any indi vidual alien if you do not like it. There will be considerable re wards for this service, and some restrictions. I know you ar interested."

"What rewards?" Lloyd asked.

"To begin with, perfect health, indefinite life, luxury of lifestyle and the permanent use of any and all artifacts of the house."

"Indefinite life?" Penn asked.

"I used that term because your length of life will be deter mined by your choice. You will have near immortality."

"But what of aging?" Chandelle asked. "Two of us are alread well toward our conclusions."

"The process is slow, but you can be restored to your youth," Abner said. "You will live, in effect, backwards, growing younge at the rate you formerly grew older, until you choose to fix on a particular age."

"Those of us who can not safely leave the house," Shree said. "What of us?"

"You will obtain the necessary identification to prove your citi zenship in any country you enter," Abner said. "You will no longer e restricted to the house, though this is with the understanding hat you will leave it in order to show aspects of the planet to lien visitors. They will wish to see both geography and history, equiring coordination of the two access portals."

"We can actually travel in time?" Penn asked.

"Only to view past scenes at particular locations. The guests nay wish to watch famous historical battles or other significant vents."

That sounded good to Penn. He would like to watch past events, without actually getting involved in them. But he had a quesion: "What about the future settings? How are they possible?"

"They are not true future scenes," Abner said. "They are nockups of likely future history, with one alien culture represented."

"The worm village!" Chandelle said.

"Yes. We used their symbol script for the instructions, as it is most readily understood by other minds. So it seemed fair to show a sample vermicular settlement. There are no physical worms there, of course."

"But there is something," Lloyd said. "Down in the big tubes. We heard it."

Abner considered. "There shouldn't be. Unless some Earthly creature managed to get in, like a rat."

"Or a crocodile," Lloyd said.

"The work was done by a subcontractor," Abner agreed. "I suppose something could have been left behind. That will bear checking out."

Lloyd wasn't the only one who nodded. That venture into the darkness had not been fun.

"Can we make friends with the aliens?" Llynn asked.

"This is encouraged. They will much prefer friendly hosts. They will be glad to share their cultures and philosophies with you. You must, however, be on guard against romantic attachments with guests, as there can be no physical contact."

There was general laughter. Romance with the types of aliens Llynn and Lloyd had described would be unlikely, however compatible they might be intellectually. But Lloyd had had just enough experience meeting aliens to know that the right ones might be quite appealing, independent of their alien metabolisms.

"This promises to be endlessly interesting," Kailash said.

"Yes," Abner said, "I regard it as the galaxy's most interesting employment."

"How about juveniles like me, who have to go home and school and all?" Lloyd asked.

"You will arrange to move to this house, where your education will be completed by mental conditioning during your sleep. You will have no further formal education unless you wish it."

"Sold!" Lloyd cried jubilantly.

"What about Obsidian?" Llynn asked.

"She may join you, subject to similar cautions."

"What are the other conditions?" Kailash asked.

"You must tell no native of Earth of the nature of this house, or allow any to discover it, unless that native is a recruit to serve in this house. You may not compromise the security of this station. You may not harm an alien guest by leading it into any distasteful situation. You may not reveal the benefits that set you apart, such as your health."

"No doctors?" Lloyd asked.

"That is correct. You may not seek to profit by your association with this house, or to bring any native here unless that native has been duly approved. You must protect yourselves with the shield at all times when away from the house. –The other conditions are similar."

"And there are further rewards?" Shree asked.

"You will be entitled to visit other tourist stations on other planets, and to cultivate alien acquaintances. You will have access to all the knowledge of the universe you that care to assimilate. There may be other benefits of similar scope."

But Penn was not satisfied. "How did this house come to be? Vas there an alien landing on Earth?"

"Not as such. A small space vessel did land, bringing a rather pecial mote of dust. It contained the pattern that enables a sapi-nt mind to expand into universal consciousness."

"The ring!" Llynn exclaimed.

"The pattern is embedded in that ring," Abner agreed. "The article landed by chance near the residence of an out of work aborer. —He picked up the remnant of the tiny ship, and his onsciousness expanded. An alien mind proffered him a deal: he knowledge and power of the universe, in exchange for per-nanently hosting the alien's mind. With this knowledge, in the ourse of a decade, he became highly successful and wealthy, hen turned his assets to the formation of a global network of iousing sites. He was given alien science to fashion devices un-nown on Earth. Then, with the continuing guidance of the alien nind, he turned to the recruitment of additional natives. I am hat man, and you six are the first recruits. Assuming that you re still interested."

Penn looked around the room, catching the eye of each of the others in turn. "We are still interested," he said.

"I have been unable to visit alien worlds myself," Abner said. "Because I could not risk any one moment of inattention until my job was complete. Hereafter, if one of you will watch my body, I will on occasion be touring myself. This is the most immediate benefit your acceptance brings me: my retirement. I will now at last be free to seek a female companion of my own. Otherwise, I will not intrude on your portion of the house."

"What of your alien resident?" Penn asked."He, too, will be able to retire and return to his home. It has been a long and at times difficult tour, but now we are ready to pass it along to the next generation. To you."

"To us," Chandelle agreed. "We will try not to disappoint you."

"You have not disappointed me. Many prospects before you

did not work out, but from the first you did. I watched and helpe
wherever I could, touching the minds of those who might hel
you." –Abner glanced at Kailash and Shree. "But you will be th
ones to select future recruits, using similar techniques. It will a
times be a challenge."

"We look forward to it," Penn said.

Shree squeezed Lloyd's hand. Her problem, and his, had jus
been solved. They would remain in the house. He knew that thi
was just the beginning.

THE END

9-99

9 781584 450009